MURDER AT A FUNERAL

THE KITTY WORTHINGTON MYSTERIES, BOOK 9

MAGDA ALEXANDER

HEARTS AFIRE PUBLISHING

CAST OF CHARACTERS

Kitty Worthington - Our amateur sleuth

The Worthington Family

    Mildred Worthington - Kitty's mother
    Edward Worthington - Kitty's father
    Ned Worthington - Kitty's oldest brother
    Richard Worthington - Kitty's next older brother
    Margaret Dalrymple - Kitty's older sister, married to Sebastian, the Duke of Wynchcombe

The Worthington Household

    Carlton - The family butler
    Mrs. Simpson - The family housekeeper
    Sir Winston - Basset Hound and beloved family pet

The Wynchcombe Family

Sebastian Dalrymple - The Duke of Wynchcombe, married to Margaret, Kitty's sister

Lady Lily Dalrymple - Sebastian's sister, residing at Worthington House

The Rutledge Family

The Marquis of Rutledge

Robert Crawford Sinclair - Kitty's fiancé. Lord Rutledge's brother. A Chief Detective Inspector at Scotland Yard.

The Rutledge Castle Staff

Mister Benton - The castle butler

Mrs. Collins - The castle housekeeper

Nigel Saybrook - Lord Rutledge's attendant

Chipping Bliss Residents

Constable Merryweather - Chipping Bliss Chief Police officer

Vicar Linus Mayfield

Andrew Lawson - Curate

Mrs. Reilly - The vicar's housekeeper

Bill Poole - The victim's brother

Doctor Springwell - Village physician

Mister Sloane - Village apothecary

Mrs. Bretton - Village dressmaker

Jenny - Dressmaker's assistant

Albert Diggum - Village Undertaker

Cam Diggum - Undertaker's son

Upton Residents

Vicar Crumb
Mrs. Helena Lawson
Lettie, Mrs. Lawson's maid

Other Notable Characters

Zubair Sharif - Richard's friend and assistant
Lord Hollingsworth - A marquis and friend to both Kitty and Robert
Lady Melissande - Lord Hollingsworth's sister, residing at Worthington House
Lady Emma Carlyle - Kitty's friend and partner at the Ladies of Distinction Detective Agency
Hudson - Robert's valet

CHAPTER 1

WORTHINGTON HOUSE, MAYFAIR, LONDON

*W*ith only a few weeks to go before my wedding day, I was suffering the daily drilling from Mother about the wedding arrangements. She'd become a militant sergeant about its preparations since our return from Brighton. Not the smallest of details escaped her. As a result, I'd learned to show up at breakfast with the three-inch thick wedding book which contained the most important details of the wedding preparations. Why she insisted on going through this inquisition during our morning meal was beyond me as it tended to spoil my appetite. But maybe that was her aim as she worried I wouldn't fit into my wedding gown. Machiavellian did not begin to describe Mother's methods.

"How many responses have we received, dear?" Mother asked as I stood next to her.

I flipped open the wedding book. Quickly finding the list of responses I updated daily, I said, "Over four hundred,

1

Mother." Everyone with a connection to our family, whether noble or commoner, had been invited.

"The Marquess and Marchioness of Huntington?"

I checked the list. "They will attend."

"And the Duchess of Combercome?"

I flipped through the pages and breathed a sigh of relief when I found her name. "Her Grace will be there as well."

"What about the final fitting for your wedding gown?"

That I didn't have to look up. "Monday at ten. Along with Margaret's, Lady Emma's, and Lady Lily's." They were to be my three bridesmaids. Well, my sister Margaret would be my matron of honor since she was married.

"The floral arrangements?"

I located the flowers section in the notebook. "They will be delivered to St. Georges several hours before the ceremony."

"And the ones for Worthington House?"

As I frantically searched through my task list, a sense of doom engulfed me. Had I forgotten to order flowers for my own home?

Lady Emma, a dear friend who resided with us, cleared her throat. "You delegated that task to me, dear Kitty. A Rare Bloom will deliver them at eight. They will assist the staff in arranging them around the ballroom and the ground floor."

"Thank you, Lady Emma."

A satisfied smile blossomed across Mother's lips. "I congratulate you, Kitty. You have everything under control."

Except for the bride to be, that is, who was on the verge of a nervous collapse.

With the inquisition seemingly ended, I proceeded to help myself to the fare which beckoned so temptingly from the baseboard.

Just as I did, Lady Lily breezed into the dining room. "My apologies for my lateness. I overslept."

"No need to apologize, Lady Lily," Mother said with a soft smile. "You need your beauty rest." Being the granddaughter of a duke and affianced to my brother Ned, Lady Lily could do no wrong in Mother's eyes. But I could not be jealous of Mother's affection for her. Lady Lily was not only beautiful but sweet as could be.

"Lil, Cook prepared your favorite, Chelsea buns," Lady Mellie said from her perch at the table. She'd come to us when her chaperone broke her leg, making it impossible for the matron to shepherd Lady Mellie through her season. Lord Hollingsworth, her brother, had asked Mother to give her shelter while he found a replacement. But Mother, who was guiding Lady Lily through her debut, had determined it'd be no harder to squire about two debutantes than one. Even though the season ended months ago, Lady Mellie had never left. She'd become one of us.

A wrinkle worried Lady Lily's brow. "I don't know if I should. I need to fit into my bridesmaid's gown."

"One Chelsea bun won't hurt you, Lady Lily," I said. "Enjoy yourself."

With a giggle, she approached the sideboard and proceeded to pile food on her plate, including the favored Chelsea bun. I couldn't help but contrast her demeanor against the timid mouse who'd come to live with us. In a year's time she'd blossomed into a happy, self-assured young lady. I, for one, could not be happier for her.

Once we settled ourselves at the table, the talk between her and Lady Mellie turned to fashion as the two young ladies simply adored the topic.

Not that I was lacking in conversation. Lady Emma, who was not only my friend but my partner at the Ladies of Distinction Detective Agency, claimed my time. "When are you planning to take your wedding sabbatical?"

"Not for another two weeks. We have too much work at

the agency to leave everything up in the air, and I want to finish the two matters I'm investigating."

Just as I stopped speaking, the door to the dining room crashed open, and one of our footmen rushed in. "Mister Carlton, there's a visitor, a gentleman. He says he is—"

He didn't get to finish. A man stumbled in behind him. Pale faced, painfully thin, leaning heavily into another gentleman who was doing his level best to hold him up.

"Mother," was all he said before collapsing to the ground.

My brother Richard had finally come home.

Mother and Father flew out of their chairs and rushed toward him.

"Oh, Edward. He's not . . . he's not," Mother said as she reached Richard's side, palpable anguish in her voice.

While we all held our breaths, Father laid not quite steady fingers on my brother's neck. After an excruciating few seconds, he glanced up at Mother, clearly relieved. "No, dear. He's unconscious, that's all."

Mother dropped to her knees. "My boy, my dear sweet boy." Tears rained down her cheeks as she cradled Richard's head.

Father's gaze turned to the man who'd helped Richard into the room. "Please explain."

"I'm Zubair Sharif, Mister Worthington's assistant." The man said in perfect English, albeit with a foreign accent.

"What's wrong with my son, Mister Sharif?"

"Malaria. He came down with it a year ago. The doctor gave him quinine. And his health improved. But two weeks ago, he suffered a relapse. I was afraid . . ." He allowed the words to dangle in the air before continuing. But I could well imagine what he feared. That Richard would die. "So I brought him home."

Father placed his hand on Mister Sharif's shoulder. His throat working with emotion, he said, "Thank you."

Mister Sharif held a palm to his heart. "You're most welcome, Sir. I would not have forgiven myself if I hadn't delivered him back to his family."

"We need to call Doctor Crawley, Edward," Mother said. Although her anguish had lessened, it was still evident.

Father nodded. "Yes, of course. I'll go telephone him."

Word must have spread quickly among the staff of Richard's arrival for they had gathered outside the dining room. As Father rushed out, they cleared a path for him.

Mother glanced at them seemingly searching for someone. "Mrs. Simpson. Are you here?"

"Yes, ma'am." Our housekeeper stepped forward.

"Please prepare Mister Richard's room."

"Of course, ma'am."

"And also one for Mister Sharif."

"There's no need, Mrs. Worthington," Mister Sharif said. "I can take a room at a lodging."

Mother glanced up at him, her composure once more under control. "There's every need, young man. You brought my son back to me." Turning to Mrs. Simpson, she said. "The Cherry Blossom bedroom, please, for Mister Sharif."

"Yes, ma'am." Mrs. Simpson rushed off with several maids trailing behind her.

Mother had redecorated many of the bedchambers with an Oriental theme in mind. The Cherry Blossom bedroom was one of the most beautiful.

"I don't want my son on the floor," Mother said. "Let's move him to the drawing room." She turned to our butler. "Mister Carlton, if you please."

He signaled a couple of footmen who gently picked up Richard and carried him out of the room.

But Mother wouldn't be Mother unless she first saw to our guest's welfare. "Have you eaten, Mister Sharif?"

"There was no time to break our fast. We came to Worthington House right from the rail station."

"And thank heaven you did."

Approaching them, I said, "I'll attend to Mister Sharif, Mother, while you tend to Richard."

"Thank you, dear," she said before following the footmen to the drawing room.

I turned to the gentleman who'd delivered Richard safely to us. "We were just enjoying our breakfast, Mister Sharif. So you've arrived at a perfect time," I said trying to lighten the mood.

"Thank you." He bowed his head before he said, "I'd like to wash first, if you don't mind."

"Yes, of course." I smiled to make him feel welcome. "Will the lavatory do until we make your room ready?"

"That will be most acceptable."

I turned to the sole footman who'd remained behind as the rest of the staff had returned to their duties. "Please show Mister Sharif to the lavatory."

"Of course, Miss Worthington," he said before turning to Mister Sharif. "If you will follow me, Sir."

Once they left, my smile vanished as I dropped into my seat.

"He'll be fine, Kitty," Lady Emma said, pressing my hand. "Your parents will make sure your brother gets the best of care."

"I'm sure they will. But it is malaria." I glanced despondently at her. "There is no cure."

CHAPTER 2

A TROUBLING AILMENT

*T*hankfully, Richard regained consciousness shortly after he was carried to the drawing room which eased Mother's mind to no end. An hour later, he was transferred to his bedchamber, as he was too weak to walk much less climb stairs. But he'd insisted on a bath and clean clothes before slipping into bed. Father's valet volunteered for that duty, as he was more than happy to help him. Indeed, our entire staff eagerly awaited some task, no matter how minor, to ensure Richard received a happy homecoming.

Doctor Crawley arrived an hour later. After his thorough examination of Richard, he prescribed plenty of bed rest and nutritious food. He was no expert in malaria, however, as he only had a rudimentary knowledge of the disease. But he knew someone who was. Doctor Ross, a leading expert in malaria. By early afternoon he was at our door. While he examined Richard, the family, including my brother Ned who'd rushed over as soon as he heard about Richard's

7

arrival, anxiously waited in the drawing room to hear what he had to say.

When Doctor Ross joined us there, unfortunately, his diagnosis was not what we hoped for, although not unexpected. "He's quite ill."

Mother whimpered as she clutched Father's hand.

"But the news is not all bad, dear lady," Doctor Ross said with a kind smile. "With proper rest and nutrition, as well as dosages of quinine, he should recover."

"Thank heavens!" Mother collapsed on the sofa, her legs giving out in relief.

It was left to Father to ask a question present in all our minds. "Will he regain his full health?"

Doctor Ross carefully worded his response. "Difficult to say. May I explain?"

"Please do," Father said, placing a comforting arm around Mother's shoulders.

"Malaria is an incurable disease. He will continue to suffer relapses. As I understand from his assistant, Mister Sharif, he came down with the disease a year ago. Thankfully, he was able to get proper care at that time and recuperated. He should have returned home to London. Instead, he resumed his excavations. A relapse was bound to happen sooner or later. It's a wonder it didn't happen for almost a year."

Mother held a handkerchief to her mouth.

"He's young, strong. He'll live through this relapse. But he must never return to his former occupation. Sooner or later, the malaria will kill him if he does."

"Oh, Edward." Mother wailed clutching Father's hand.

With him busy comforting her, it was left to Ned to explore further. "What if he doesn't return to Egypt? If he remains here in London, what will happen?"

"He will have excellent care available to him which means

future relapses can be treated immediately."

"Can he lead a normal life if he remains at home?" Father asked.

"I don't see why not," Doctor Ross said with a smile. "There is hope, Mister and Missus Worthington. A great deal of research is being conducted on this disease. Illustrious minds are applying considerable efforts to developing more effective medicines and treatments. His future is not dire by any means. He will be able to marry, have children, engage in a useful occupation."

"But not in Egypt," Father said.

"No. Not in Egypt." Doctor Ross glanced at his pocket watch. "Now, I must go. I have a consultation at my surgery. I will return in three days to check his progress. In the meantime, Doctor Crawley will monitor his care. I understand he's arranged for round the clock nursing?"

"Yes. A day nurse and a night nurse," Mother said.

"He'll need it for a few days, until he's clear of this episode. But after that, he can resume his normal life pattern. Just try to keep him rested and well-fed."

I smiled. "There's no doubt of that, Doctor Ross. Mother will make sure."

"Can we see him?" Mother asked.

"Of course. I'm sure he will enjoy a visit from his family. Keep it to ten minutes and not everyone at once, though. In a few days, you will get to enjoy his company for longer periods of time."

After Doctor Ross left, we decided on the order of things. Mother and Father would go first and then Ned. Margaret and Sebastian would visit him before supper. I would bring up the rear after our evening meal.

Mother had arranged a supper party a week ago. Too late to cancel after Richard's arrival, she decided to carry through with her plans. Thankfully, the guests were all close friends who would both comprehend the gravity of the situation and rejoice in Richard's return.

"How is he?" My fiancé Robert Crawford Sinclair asked as soon as he stepped into the room that evening. Earlier in the day, I'd telephoned him at Scotland Yard to alert him to the state of things.

"He's quite exhausted, a combination of the disease and the long trip. We're taking turns visiting him. Mother, Father, and Ned went up this afternoon. Margaret and Sebastian are up there now. I'll check in with him after supper. I'd like you to meet him."

"Of course. Whatever you wish, Catherine," he said squeezing my hand.

"Did you ever come across malaria in your travels?" I asked Lord Hollingsworth when he approached. A dear friend of ours, he was an explorer who sailed around the world in search of knowledge of other cultures.

"Only once. Eager to see the Amazon River, we sailed to Brazil. But there was a malaria outbreak. We did not stay."

"Wise decision," Robert said.

"Have you met Mister Sharif, Hollingsworth?" I asked. "Richard's assistant. He brought him back to us."

"Haven't had the pleasure," he said.

"Then let me introduce you."

After having done so, I said. "Lord Hollingsworth is an explorer, Mister Sharif. He recently traveled to the South Seas."

"I would love to hear about it," Mister Sharif said. "I've never left Egypt until now."

"And I would love to hear about your excavations." As I expected, Hollingsworth did not disappoint.

Upon my return to Robert's side, he said, "Very adroitly done, Catherine."

"Thank you. They have a lot in common, so they should have plenty to talk about."

"Does Mister Sharif plan to stay or return to Egypt?"

"He hasn't said one way or another, but I hope he stays at least for a little while."

Fifteen minutes later, Carlton announced supper putting an end to our discussion. During the meal Mother purposefully kept the topic of conversation away from Richard. Not only did she wish to preserve his privacy, but she wanted to keep the talk light and cheery.

By the time Robert and I made our way to Richard's room it was close to ten.

"He needs his sleep," the nurse said, disapproval evident on her face.

"I'm quite awake, Nurse," Richard hailed from his bed. "Please allow my sister to enter."

Frowning, the nurse opened wide the door while cautioning Robert and me from taking up too much of Richard's time.

As I approached the bed, I was glad to see some color had returned to his face and a small spark of merriment shone in his eyes.

"Hello, darling," I said as I bent to kiss his cheek. "How are you feeling?"

"Fit as a fiddle." His irrepressible dimple popped up. Among all us siblings, he was the only one who possessed one. His gaze shifted to my fiancé. "This must be Robert."

"Indeed, he is. Please allow me to introduce you to Chief Detective Inspector Robert Crawford Sinclair."

Richard held out his hand. "A pleasure. I've heard plenty about you from Kitty."

"All good things, I hope," Robert replied with a grin.

Richard raised a mocking brow. "Well . . ."

"You're awful, Dickie." I teased before turning to Robert. "Of course, it was all good things."

"He arrested you, didn't he?" Dickie asked.

"*That* was a misunderstanding," I asserted.

"Was it?" Robert asked. "You were breaking and entering as I recall."

"Yes, well."

"She was always one to flout convention, even as a child," my brother said.

"I had no inkling she was such a rule breaker," Robert responded with a grin.

A blatant falsehood. Time and again, I'd acted contrary to what society expected of me. And he'd been there front and center for most of them.

"Once you've recuperated, I'd love to hear more," Robert said addressing my brother.

"Don't you dare reveal all my sins!" I warned Richard.

"Couldn't possibly reveal *all*. That would take a year or two." He straightened himself up. "So when do I get sprung from this bed? No one will tell me."

"Doctor Ross will visit in three days. He will assess your condition at that time."

Frowning, he dropped his head back on his pillow. "An eternity."

"I'll come and read to you if you wish."

"Oh, not that." He sat up once more. "I need a diversion not be put to sleep."

"That's the thanks I get for offering my very valuable time," I scoffed. "Very well, what would you enjoy?"

"I heard music," Richard said. "A piano?"

"Lady Mellie." I quickly explained who she was and why she was residing with us.

"She plays like an angel," Richard said.

"Looks like one too. No one could deny Lady Mellie's red-haired, blue-eyed beauty.

That perked him up. "Does she really?"

Seeing his interest, I asked, "Would you like to meet her?"

The nurse cleared her throat. "I'm afraid your visit must come to a close. Mister Worthington must get his rest."

"Bring Lady Mellie," Richard said. "Tomorrow after breakfast. Say ten o'clock."

"I will. Goodnight, Dickie." Leaning over, I kissed a cheek that felt cold and clammy. He might be putting up a good front, but he was ill. Seriously ill. I prayed he would truly recuperate. We'd already lost one sibling to the Spanish Flu. Mother would not survive the loss of another child.

CHAPTER 3

ROBERT HAS NEWS

After leaving Richard's room, we headed toward the drawing room with the aim of rejoining family and guests. But along the way, Robert made a request.

"Is there somewhere we could have a private word?"

"Yes, of course. The library should do." In past times, we'd held many a sensitive conversation there.

Once we reached it, I put my arms around his waist. "Was this your way of arranging an opportunity to kiss me?"

His glance which usually was quite amused when I made such a remark turned melancholic. "No. Not this time."

"Oh?" I stepped away. His serious look concerned me.

"My brother."

"Lord Rutledge." I'd known Robert as the adopted son of a London couple who'd showered him with love and affection. But as it turned out, Lord Rutledge's father had married a local woman from his village and their union had borne fruit in Robert, making him Lord Rutledge's brother. But Robert's birth parents had both died—she in childbirth, he of a heart condition—before Robert could be claimed as their son.

Many years later, birth and marriage certificates had been discovered by Lord Rutledge's new man of business. Once he learned about the existence of a lost brother, Lord Rutledge hired a detective to find him. After doing so, Lord Rutledge had sponsored Robert through Oxford and encouraged him to work for Scotland Yard, rather than as a policeman which had been Robert's profession.

Lord Rutledge kept his familial connection from Robert until his adoptive parents died. But once he informed Robert of his true parentage, he'd transferred property and funds to him. Only a few months ago, Lord Rutledge revealed to our family that Robert was the heir to the Rutledge title and estate. To say we were surprised was an understatement. At the same time, we were extremely happy for both Lord Rutledge and Robert as the title would not go extant, and the estate would transfer to a living heir. But it seemed that now there was something that concerned Lord Rutledge. "Is anything wrong?"

"He wishes to reinter the remains of my birth mother next to our father's in the Rutledge Castle cemetery. He believes it's the proper thing to do."

"Oh!" This was literally the last thing I thought he would say. The thought had never once crossed my mind. "When does he wish this to take place?"

"In four days." He held my hands and kissed their fingertips. "I know the timing is perfectly awful with your brother just returned. But I will be gone for only a short while. I should return in plenty of time for our wedding."

"Don't be silly, darling." Freeing one hand, I cupped his cheek. "We won't be apart. I'm coming with you."

His brow wrinkled. "Are you sure? Your family, Richard, may need you here."

"I love my family, but you are my husband to be." I curled my arms around his waist once more and nestled against his broad chest. "I won't desert you in your hour of need."

The tension in him eased as he laid his head on top of mine. "I must admit I'm glad you're coming. It will be easier with you there."

"It's only for a few days, Robert. Once we've paid our respects to your mother, we will return to London so you can participate in the events leading up to our ceremony."

"Anything in particular?" He asked in a suspicious tone.

"Well." Putting a bit of space between us, I peeked up at him through my eyelashes. "I believe Hollingsworth is planning something."

"Such as?"

"As I'm a mere female, he hasn't shared it with me. But at Brighton, I spotted him in deep conversation with Marlowe, Ned, and Sebastian. From their shifty glances, I suspected something clandestine. When I walked toward them to hear what they were saying, they became deadly silent, but I definitely heard the word kidnap. I just hope you don't get arrested. I would hate to be lacking a groom on my wedding day."

Laughing, he pulled me into him. "No chance of that. I know people in Scotland Yard."

"Yes, well, there is that," I said before he thoroughly kissed me. As I intended, his melancholic mood all but vanished.

When we rejoined our family and friends, I didn't share Robert's news with them. We thought it would be better to wait until the next day to approach Mother. She had enough on her plate today. My news could wait.

∾

WHEN I TOLD her the next morning, she decried the timing. Something not entirely unexpected. But she agreed it was the right thing for me to accompany Robert.

"Such a shame his birth parents didn't get to see Robert grow up."

"Undoubtedly, but he had a happy upbringing. The Crawfords were wonderful parents."

For a few seconds, she scrutinized me. Probably wondering how to best phrase her next question. It wasn't the first time I'd witnessed that look. "Does he ever talk about them?" She finally asked.

"Only when I inquire about them. He almost never volunteers any information on his own."

"Robert feels deeply, but it's something he finds hard to express. Like most men."

"He never fails to show his love for me," I rightfully pointed out.

"Yes, I know, dear," Mother replied with a knowing smile. "Of that, I'm certain."

"We've never done anything untoward," I rushed to say.

"Not for your lack of trying, young lady." Her voice took on a harder tone. "You'd tempt a saint with your antics."

My face flared up with heat. How could she know what I'd asked of Robert at Brighton? Not that it got me anywhere. "He turned me down."

"I would expect no less of him. He is an honorable man."

With that I had to agree.

"Kitty, my dear. He'll be in a vulnerable state at Castle Rutledge. His mother's funeral is bound to take an emotional toll on him. Support him in his hour of need. But whatever you do, don't ask more than he can give."

"I won't."

"Good." She nodded her approval. "Now, have you visited your brother today?"

Happy to move away from the sadder topic, I said, "Not yet. I wanted to talk to you first about my travel plans."

"He's eager to meet Lady Mellie. Her music is a source of comfort for him."

Maybe so, but I could see the wheels turning in her head. "And you hope she proves an incentive for his remaining in London."

A small smile flitted across her mouth. "I have to admit I do. Lady Mellie is beautiful, educated, unattached. I can't help but think they'd make a perfect couple. It is so wrong of me to hope for such a thing?"

"Of course not, dearest." I kissed her cheek. "But he'll want more than true love to keep him in London. He'll need something to keep his mind occupied."

"Your father has an idea about that. But much as I press him, he won't reveal what it is unless it bears fruit. He doesn't want me to feel disappointed if it falls through."

Or maybe he thought she'd let something slip before it could be arranged. Mother could keep secrets, as I well knew. But something that would relate to Richard remaining in London might be too much for her to keep confidential. The prospect of it was indeed a happy one, and I couldn't help but rejoice. "I hope he succeeds. It would be wonderful to have Dickie permanently home."

She let out a soft sigh. "Yes, it would be. Now go find Lady Mellie."

It didn't take any detective skills to find her. I just had to follow the sound of the melody that streamed from the music room.

"Good morning, Lady Mellie!"

The tune came to a stop. "I'm not bothering, am I? Sometimes I get carried away."

"On the contrary, your music is a balm to anyone who

hears it, especially Dickie. Last night he shared how much he loved your piano renderings."

"Oh." The pink in her cheeks lent a lovely glow to her milk and roses complexion.

"In fact, he would very much like to meet you."

"Now?" A look of dismay spread over her face.

"Yes. It's not a problem, is it?"

"Oh, no. It's just"—she glanced down, apparently scrutinizing what she was wearing—"this gown is not suitable for visits." Being a fashion aficionado, Lady Mellie owned gowns for different purposes. The one she was wearing would be classified as an at-home dress.

"You don't have to. It's perfectly lovely. But if you'd like to change, I will await you outside his room in say, fifteen minutes?"

"Yes, thank you." And with that she rushed off.

At the agreed upon time, she joined me outside of Richard's room dressed in a sleeveless blue chiffon gown with a sash tied low around her hips. For her jewelry, she'd chosen a pearl necklace and a matching pair of earrings her brother had gifted her.

"It's not too much, is it?" Lady Mellie asked.

"Dickie will be enchanted." Of that, I had no doubt.

After a soft knock on his door, a nurse answered. Thankfully, she was a different one from last night's battle ax.

"Hello. I'm Kitty Worthington, and this is Lady Melissande. We're here to visit Richard. Is he awake?"

Before the nurse could say a word, Richard's voice reached us. "I most certainly am and bored to flinders. Where the devil have you . . .?" His voice died out as he caught sight of Lady Mellie. "Hello." He'd been allowed to leave his bed and was now seated by a round table in the center of the room.

As we joined him there, I said, "Richard, may I present Lady Melissande? She goes by Lady Mellie."

Somehow, he managed to reach her hand and kiss it. "How very pleasant to meet you, Lady Mellie. Are you the angel who's been playing the piano?"

Lady Mellie's face pinked up. "I don't know about being an angel, but, yes, I've been playing. Do you like it?"

"I'm enchanted."

Exactly as I thought.

"I'm sorry to interrupt," the nurse said, "Doctor Crawley would like visits held to ten minutes."

"How about fifteen?" I asked. "Lady Mellie and Richard need to get acquainted."

An understanding smile flitted across her lips. "Very well, but no more than that." She wasn't the martinet the night nurse was.

"Go away, Kitty," Richard said in the next instant.

"Yes, Dickie." I walked out of the room secure in the knowledge my mission had been accomplished. The falling in love part? Well, that would be up to them.

CHAPTER 4

A TRAIN JOURNEY

*W*hen Doctor Ross visited that afternoon, he was surprised to find Richard had greatly improved. So much so that he cleared him to join the family for breakfast and supper. Of course, Richard being Richard did not stop at that. The next day, he also wandered about the house reacquainting himself with the household. He'd always been a favorite of the kitchen staff, so he visited for a cuppa and biscuits while Cook filled him in on all the gossip.

Mother, of course, had her spies. When Richard's energy flagged, she magically appeared at his side and ordered him back to bed. He grumbled, of course, but did as he was told. That evening, after his respite, he joined us for supper. We were all glad to see him and rejoiced in his ability to remain with us this much.

After the meal ended, he beseeched Lady Mellie for a melody or two. She, of course, was happy enough to oblige. They proceeded to the music room on their own, while the rest of the family remained in the drawing room. No chaperone was needed when we could easily hear her play. As he'd had no access to the music revolution that had occurred during the last several years, he was fascinated by the newer compositions, especially the jazz ones. She would have played endlessly for him that evening. But after an hour or so, Mother put a stop to it, declaring Lady Mellie needed her rest.

By supper the next day, it was clear Dickie was growing restless. After the meal ended, we congregated in the drawing room. That's when Father suggested a sojourn to a place my brother had found fascinating years ago.

"You haven't visited the British Museum for some time, Richard. As I understand it, their collection of ancient artifacts has grown quite considerably. You might want to visit."

Richard raised a questioning brow. "Father, is this your way of pushing me out of the nest?"

"Not at all, son. I'm merely suggesting an excursion I believe you'd enjoy."

"But only for the morning or afternoon, Richard," Mother cautioned. "Mister Sharif can accompany you to make sure you don't tire."

Mister Sharif glanced up at that comment. "I would be glad to do so, Mrs. Worthington. I'd love to see the museum's extensive Egyptian collection."

"There you are, Richard," Mother said.

"Yes, Mother." His answer was all that was proper, but I could tell he resented the reference to his physical weakness. "I believe I shall turn in."

A chorus of voices bid him goodnight.

As the next day Robert and I were headed to Chipping Bliss early in the morning, I wanted to say goodbye to him. But in private, as I had something I wished to say. "I'll walk with you if you don't mind."

"Of course not." He winged an arm, and I curled my arm around it. Together, we slowly climbed the stairs.

When we reached my door, he said, "I like Robert. He's a good egg."

"He is." I placed my hand on his chest. "Dickie. While I'm gone, I want you to listen to what Mother and Father have to say. They mean the best for you."

"They want me to stay in London."

"Can you blame them? Egypt is no longer a good place for you."

He dipped his head to hide the misery in his eyes. "I know. But I'm a man of action, Kitty. A leopard cannot change his spots."

"There are plenty of occupations in London that will keep you busy. Look at me. I'm constantly on the go."

His dimple popped through. "Maybe I'll become a detective and join your agency."

"Afraid you don't qualify," I quipped.

He frowned. "Why not?"

"Because it's the *Ladies* of Distinction Detective Agency."

"What about Mister Clapham? Yes, I know all about him."

"He's a consultant, not an employee."

He lowered his brow. "Splitting hairs, sister dear."

He was right. "Umm, maybe until you find something that interests you."

"And have my younger sister as my boss?" He shuddered dramatically. "Heaven forbid."

"In all seriousness, Dickie, you can find something to occupy you in London."

"If you say so," he sounded downright despondent. With a last hug and a kiss to my cheek, he said, "Goodbye, old bean. Say hello to Robert for me."

"I will."

Without another word, he wandered off toward his room.

I thought the thorny problem that was Richard would keep me awake, but I was so exhausted it took no time to fall asleep.

UNFORTUNATELY, a matter came up at Scotland Yard the following morning that Robert needed to handle, so we were not able to depart until early afternoon. After Robert collected me, we headed to Paddington where we would take the train to Moreton on Marsh. There we would be met by Lord Rutledge's chauffeur who would drive us to Rutledge Castle near the village of Chipping Bliss. The train ride was not long. A little over an hour and a half. But during that time, I could see Robert was troubled.

"What is it, darling?" I asked slipping my hand into his.

"What?"

"Your mind is a million miles away. What's troubling you?"

"The reinterment. It feels strange. I know that I should feel something. She was my birth mother after all."

"You are feeling something."

"Yes, I am. Regret that I never met her, or my father for that matter. But at least my brother has told me enough tales about him that I feel I know him. But he knows nothing about my birth mother. No tales, no stories that he can share with me. He doesn't even know what she looked like. I will be burying a stranger." He glanced off into the distance. "And that is so unfair to her. Someone should remember her for who she was. After all, the marquis loved her enough to marry her."

"Your father."

"My birth father, yes."

"But you consider your real father to be Mister Crawford and his wife your mother."

"They raised me. They loved me. If it hadn't been for them . . ."

"You would have grown up in an orphanage." And unfortunately, those places tended not to be the best. We'd seen what one had done to the daughter of one of our friends. Lavender Rose did not even speak when we first met her at the tender age of six. And she'd been raised in a facility that truly cared for their children.

"Yes."

I rubbed his shoulder. "Everything you are feeling, Robert. It's natural. Torn between two sets of parents. One who gave birth to you, another who raised you. You want to know what I think?"

"Please."

"They made you, all of them. Your birth parents gave you life. Your adoptive parents raised you. From everything I've heard, they were good people. I think they're all smiling down on you. Proud and happy of the man you've become."

"You always know the right thing to say. I love you."

He leaned over to kiss me just as the train conductor approached our compartment. "Moreton on Marsh our next stop."

"That's us," I said.

"Yes, it is."

He came to his feet and grabbed our bags from the overhead shelf. As we stepped onto the Moreton on Marsh train station platform, we had no idea of what awaited us or the many days we would end up spending at Castle Rutledge.

CHAPTER 5

CASTLE RUTLEDGE

At the Moreton on Marsh rail station, we were met by Lord Rutledge's chauffeur who promptly took possession of our luggage and stowed it in the Rolls Royce, Lord Rutledge's automobile. Barely half an hour later, we arrived at our destination. Built on the ruins of a previous foundation, the square structure with towers at all four ends was at least 500 years old. Motifs of the Italianate style had been added in the 19th century, especially its towers when the castle had been redesigned in the Jacobethan style.

I squeezed Robert's arm as we rode up to the gate. "It's quite imposing, isn't it?"

"Yes, that it is." His voice carried both awe and dismay which didn't surprise me. He hadn't been born with a silver spoon in his mouth. So, he'd never expected to inherit a centuries old castle. And that was bound to be a heavy responsibility.

"It is a lot to take in," I said.

He nodded.

As he helped me from the vehicle, I joined our hands. "We'll make it work, Robert. You're not alone."

He shot me a loving glance. "I'm very grateful you're by my side, Catherine. I'm glad you came."

"And so you should be," I joked to lighten the mood.

He acknowledged my message by squeezing my hand.

Without further ado, we made our way past the castle gate to the entrance hall. With its high vaulted ceilings, intricate stonework, and vast floor space, it could have been rather austere. But the warm hues to the winged chairs, sofas, and rugs we spotted lent a congenial air to the castle. This message was reinforced by the grand welcoming committee that awaited us. Lord Rutledge stood front and center, his attendant behind him. In recent months, Robert's brother had grown weaker from his heart condition and now depended on his manservant to move about. But the two of them were not the only ones present. The entire castle staff stood to the right of him.

Leaning heavily on his cane, Lord Rutledge embraced Robert and me. "Welcome to Castle Rutledge."

"Thank you, Sir," Robert said.

"It's quite beautiful, your lordship."

"Thank you, my dear. But let's hear what you have to say after you've suffered through some of its deficiencies. It can be a drafty old thing. But at least we have hot and cold running water and modern plumbing."

I laughed as he intended me to.

He pointed to the man standing next to him. With more grey than black in his hair and as tall as Robert, he was a commanding figure. "This is Mister Benton, butler extraordinaire. He keeps the castle running like a Swiss watch."

"How do you do, Mister Benton?" I asked.

"As fine as can be, Lord Robert, Miss Worthington." The

butler said, inclining his head. "If I can be of any service, all you need do is ask."

Lord Rutledge continued down the line. "And this is Mrs. Collins, our housekeeper."

Dressed in black and middling in height, she appeared to be in her fifties. Her hair had been arranged in braids, the silver blending beautifully with the gold.

"If there's something amiss in your room," Lord Rutledge said, "she will be more than happy to assist."

"Indeed, your lordship," Mrs. Collins said as she curtsied. "I understand you did not bring your maid with you, Miss Worthington."

"No. My wedding trousseau is arriving daily, so she's needed back home."

"I've assigned Annie to assist you." She waved a hand, and a smiling young woman stepped forward and curtsied.

"Miss."

"She's been properly trained as a lady's maid. So you need not worry."

"I'm sure Annie will be splendid." I smiled at her.

"Ta, Miss."

"That's all for now, Benton," Lord Rutledge said.

"Of course, your lordship," the butler responded. A single flick of his fingers, and the staff drifted away.

Having introduced us to the main staff members, Lord Rutledge turned to walk deeper into the castle. As he did, he pointed to the right. "The great hall. Never eat there if I can help it. Too drafty for these old bones. The library is over there." He pointed to the left. "Filled to the brim with dusty old tomes nobody reads."

Directly in front of us was a huge open space, furnished with sofas, settees and chairs.

"The saloon. Used for receptions and such. The bedrooms

are on the first floor." A sweeping staircase to our right led the way there.

"How perfectly splendid, Lord Rutledge."

"Glad it meets with your favor." He turned to Mister Benton. "I trust our supper is ready."

"Yes, your lordship. In the small drawing room as you requested."

"And the fireplace has been lit?"

"As you wished."

Lord Rutledge turned to me. "The fireplace will warm you right up, my dear."

"That's very kind of you to notice, your lordship." After the half hour drive from the train station, never mind the drafty air of the castle, my feet, never mind my nose, were numb.

"You'll need to dress in layers, Kitty, if you don't want to freeze," he stated.

"Duly noted, Sir." I had packed a warmer wardrobe. However, I had not worn them on my journey. A mistake I would not make again.

"You should have said something," Robert said as he unbuttoned his jacket and draped it over me. "Better?"

"Yes, thank you," I said reveling in the warmth of the jacket and the scent of him. As we entered the drawing room, the heat from the fireplace enveloped me, and I sighed in relief.

"Ahhh," Lord Rutledge said. "Drinks first, Benton. And then we can enjoy our hearty meal." Turning to me, he said. "You'll get your first taste of Castle Rutledge Reserve, my dear."

"Oh?" I half asked, half wondered.

"We make it ourselves. Didn't Robert tell you? We have our own brewery."

"No, he didn't." I shot Robert a grin. "It must have slipped his mind." Although how he'd forgotten to tell me about a brewery on the Rutledge estate was beyond me. Still, there was no use teasing him about it.

"I'm glad you accompanied Robert, Kitty. It will give you a chance to acquaint yourself with the Castle Rutledge estate and its staff. Robert has visited in the past, so he's learned a fair bit. But there's so much more he needs to know."

That statement did not surprise me. After all, Robert had not been formally acknowledged as the heir to the title and the Castle Rutledge estate until a few months ago. He'd tried to acquaint himself with everything that pertained to his responsibility. But his work at Scotland Yard kept him much too occupied to learn it all.

But it was something Robert needed to do sooner rather than later. Lord Rutledge joked about being at death's door. Unfortunately, he was right. His health was not good. Not too long ago, he'd suffered a heart attack which had caused him to reassess his life expectancy and determine what needed to be done. The reinterment of Robert's mother was one of those things. Robert and my wedding was another. He wanted to live long enough to see his brother married, and that date was mere weeks away. I dreaded to think what would happen to him once the ceremony was held.

"You as well, Kitty," Lord Rutledge said. "One day you will be the Lady of this castle."

"Yes, Your Lordship." I might as well start asking questions. "Do you employ the dining hall for more formal events?"

"I used to. But I no longer do. I prefer the cozy atmosphere of the drawing room. It's easier to keep warm than the dining hall. Unless it's summer, the dishes tend to grow cold rather quickly."

Something to keep in mind if Robert ever planned to entertain at the castle when he became Lord Rutledge. I couldn't see him having a shooting party in autumn, though, like so many aristocrats did. Not only had he been raised in London, but he hadn't ever attended that sort of event. I couldn't see him having one in the future.

"The dining hall fireplace is twelve feet across and tall enough for a man to stand in," Lord Rutledge further explained. "It takes a prodigious amount of firewood to heat up."

My heart sank. Did the rest of the castle depend on fireplaces to keep everyone warm? "How are the bedrooms heated?"

"With radiators. Of course, we still have the fireplaces in case additional heating is needed."

I breathed a sigh of relief.

"Rutledge Castle can be quite cold during the dearth of winter. That's why I remain in London during those months."

Once we finished our meal, he suggested Robert show me the gallery.

"That's a splendid idea," I said.

With the funeral set for the next day, I would only have this evening to acquaint myself with the castle. It was truly splendorous, although in a different way from Wynchcombe Castle, the edifice that belonged to Sebastian, my sister Margaret's husband, the Duke of Wynchcombe. That structure was so large that, if you wandered along the corridors, you might very well get lost.

"If you'll forgive me, my dear," Lord Rutledge said, "I believe it's time for me to turn in." He needed his rest before facing the rigors of the funeral the next day.

"Of course, Sir," I said. "Good night."

Robert echoed my sentiment.

Lord Rutledge had wired the castle for electricity, so we were not in the dark as we roamed the picture gallery which was about 300 hundred feet in length. Portraits of Rutledge ancestors hung on the walls. We met the first, the second, the third until we ended at the next to last. "This is Lord Rutledge's father, the eighth Marquis Rutledge."

I did not expect what I saw. "Good heavens, Robert! You're the spitting image of him." Same dark hair and eyes, same demeanor. Same roguish smile. The artist had captured the marquis at approximately the same age Robert was now.

"Yes, I rather resemble him."

"Resemble? He could be your twin!" No wonder Lord Rutledge had never doubted Robert's parentage. But then he could have been illegitimate. The birth certificate put paid to that notion, though. A dutiful midwife had completed it. And, of course, the marriage certificate between Lord Rutledge and Robert's mother, verified that he had been conceived during the time of their short-lived union. Robert's brother had hired a solicitor and filed papers before the courts to certify Robert was his true heir. In every way possible, Robert had been legitimized.

Another painting down the gallery depicted a tall gentleman with two young boys standing next to him. A dog at his feet. "Who's that?"

"My grandfather."

"And the two boys?"

"My father is the taller one. His brother William is the other."

"I didn't know you had an uncle."

"I don't. Unfortunately, he died in the second Boer War."

Another painting showed a couple dressed in the mode of Victorian times. "Your grandparents?"

"Yes. My brother rather resembles her."

"He does, while you resemble your father."

After walking the length of the gallery, we turned back. As we did, I said, "Lord Rutledge's health seems to have grown worse." Last time I'd seen him was before we left for Brighton. He'd seemed heartier then than he appeared today.

His gaze grew bleak. "His heart is growing weaker. His doctor informed me he may not last the year."

Wishing to offer what comfort I could, I rested my hand on his arm. "I'm so sorry, Robert. I was not aware."

"He does not wish it to be known."

"He will return with us to London after the funeral? He shouldn't be left alone."

"I don't intend to leave him behind."

Exhaustion suddenly claimed me, and I yawned.

"I believe it's time you sought your bed."

"It has been a rather long day." And tomorrow was bound to be exhausting.

He escorted me to the room I'd been assigned—the Lady's Chamber. To my surprise, he walked into the room with me. My surprise must have shown on my face because he rushed to explain. "There are some things I wish to discuss."

What it could be, I had no idea.

"From this point forward, this will be your bedchamber."

Of course, it would. Why would I change rooms? And then it dawned on me what he meant. "After we marry, you mean?"

"Yes."

I glanced around to take in the space. The huge room held a four-poster bed and a seating arrangement around a fireplace that was unlit. Thankfully, it didn't need to be. The room was toasty warm thanks to the radiator in the corner. But even though this was the Lady's Chamber, I doubted I would sleep here in the future. We'd already decided we'd share the same bed after our wedding day. "Where will you be?"

"In the Lord's Chamber. Three rooms separate us—a bathing chamber and our two dressing rooms."

"So we share a bath but have our own dressing areas?"

"Antiquated, I know. The castle was built when water had to be carried up flights of stairs. It made things easier for the servants to deal with only one bathtub. Plumbing has now been installed so that's no longer necessary, but the arrangement remains. I hope you don't mind."

I grinned. "Of course not. I think it's rather charming."

"Now, about tomorrow. Annie will bring you breakfast at eight which should provide you with sufficient time to bathe and dress."

"Absolutely. What about you?"

"The same, except I'll start my day an hour earlier. We'll leave for the church at ten. The funeral will take place at eleven. The vicar and the curate will be there along with the organist and the funeral director. Since this is a private ceremony, no one else will be present."

And then, rather abruptly, he pulled me into his arms, kissed me, and said goodnight.

CHAPTER 6

AN UNWELCOME GUEST

*T*he day of the funeral dawned bright and clear and much warmer than the day before. I enjoyed the breakfast in bed that Annie brought to me. After bathing, I slipped into the dress I'd chosen for the funeral. A simple design. Nothing ornate about it. But it would keep me warm as it was made from black wool crepe. Black gloves and shoes completed the ensemble. I decided against the coat I'd brought. Given the warmer temperatures, my white fur stole would serve better. The only adornments I wore were a black pearl necklace, matching pearl earrings, and my emerald and diamond engagement ring.

At a quarter to ten I descended the stairs and went in search of Robert. I found him and Lord Rutledge waiting for me in the drawing room.

Robert suggested a tot of whiskey to brace me for what was to come. Rather early in the day for spirits, but I drank it. One never knew what fortification would be needed. And then we proceeded to the Rolls Royce where Lord Rutledge's chauffeur waited for us.

It took but fifteen minutes to reach Chipping Bliss where around a thousand souls lived. Before reaching the church, we drove past what appeared to be the heart of the town. A butcher, a baker, a pub, a dress shop, and a bakery were all represented. But no one was in the streets.

Strange to say the least. But then I wasn't familiar with villages. Other than my one-year stint in a Swiss finishing school, I'd lived all my life in London, a city always teeming with people.

When we arrived at the church, Lord Rutledge's attendant helped him out of the automobile. As they slowly made their way to the Norman-style church, I expected to see the vicar. But, strangely enough, he wasn't there.

"Odd," Lord Rutledge said. "Vicar Mayfield should be here to welcome us."

"Maybe he's waiting inside, Sir," Robert suggested.

"Yes, yes, of course." But Lord Rutledge sounded unsure. More than likely, they'd arranged to meet at the entrance.

The vicar was not in the nave. Another gentleman was, however. Tall, thin as a rail, a lugubrious expression on his face. The undertaker as it turned out.

"Will Diggum, the undertaker," Lord Rutledge offered by way of explanation. "Mister Diggum, this is my brother Lord Robert Crawford Sinclair, and his fiancée, Catherine Worthington."

Once we exchanged pleasantries, the undertaker introduced the young man standing next to him. "My son. Cam."

Cam pulled on his forelock. "Your worships."

"I've taken care of all the arrangements, exactly as you asked, Your Lordship."

"Thank you," Lord Rutledge said. "Have you seen Vicar Mayfield?"

"No, milord." He fiddled with his starched collar. "I expected him a half hour ago."

Before Lord Rutledge could comment on the vicar's absence, another gentleman stumbled forward. "Joe Houghton. The organist." He belched loudly and then dropped face forward on the stone floor.

"Good heavens," I exclaimed. "He's drunk."

"Something's not right," Robert said. He turned to Lord Rutledge's manservant. "Nigel, please escort Lord Rutledge to the front pew and keep him company while Miss Worthington and I search the church."

"Of course, Lord Robert." As the presumptive heir and Lord Rutledge's brother, Robert was entitled to that courtesy title.

"Mister Diggum, have your son help the organist to one of the back pews."

"Yes, of course." The undertaker turned to his son. "Go on. Do as his lordship says."

Cam was a big, hefty lad and the organist was rather puny looking, so it took no effort for him to get the organist to his feet. Having done so, he dropped him rather unceremoniously into one of the back pews.

Once Lord Rutledge was accommodated in the front, we left him to Nigel's care. And then Robert and I went in search of the vicar.

"Where should we look first?" I asked.

"The sacristy." The room where the vicar would have donned his vestments before conducting a service.

We knocked just to be cautious. After all, we didn't want to catch him while he was changing clothes. When no one answered, Robert cautiously opened the door. The light from one of the windows softly illuminated a white-haired figure sitting in an elaborately decorated armchair, its back to us.

"Vicar Mayfield," Robert called out. "Sir."

When he didn't answer, I said, "Maybe he's fallen asleep."

"Odd thing to do when you have a funeral to conduct." Stepping closer to the still figure, Robert called out again, "Vicar Mayfield."

We continued walking forward until we reached the seated figure. The person was no gentleman, but a lady. And she was quite still.

"Oh, good heavens," I exclaimed. "She's not dead, is she?"

Robert put his fingers to her pulse at the base of her neck. After a few seconds, he said, "Afraid so."

"She's wearing the vicar's vestments." Nothing like stating the obvious. "Why would that be? And where is the vicar?"

"Haven't the foggiest." He glanced around the room. So did I for that matter, but there was no one else to be found.

"The entire church will need to be searched," Robert said. "But not by us. We'll need to fetch the constable."

"Maybe the undertaker's son can take on that task?"

He nodded. "What an awful mess."

I felt for him. A difficult situation had become even more so. But at least we would not be required to investigate whatever had happened here. That would be left to the local police. Unfortunately, I was quite wrong.

CHAPTER 7

CONSEQUENCES

"*D*id you locate the vicar?" A disgruntled Lord Rutledge asked when we returned to his side.

"Afraid not, Sir," Robert answered. "We discovered a dead woman in the sacristy dressed in the vicar's vestments."

"A woman? Who?" Lord Rutledge bit out.

"I don't know. Mister Diggum might recognize her. But I prefer to let the village constable sort this out."

"Yes, of course. We don't want you, or Kitty, caught up in this." Turning around to face the back of the church, Lord Rutledge cried out to the undertaker, "You, Sir. We need to fetch the village constable."

The undertaker rushed forward until he was standing next to us. "Why?"

"I'm afraid we found the dead body of a woman in the sacristy," Robert explained.

Mister Diggum's eyes widened. "Never say. Who?"

39

"As I'm not familiar with the inhabitants of this village, I can't identify her."

"Want me to look?" Mister Diggum appeared eager to perform that task. But then he was an undertaker. He was accustomed to seeing dead bodies.

Robert, however, disallowed him of that notion. "I prefer we wait until the village constable arrives. Maybe your son can go to the constabulary and inform him we need his assistance?"

"Of course." Mister Diggum turned around and yelled out to his son who was loitering in the back of the church enjoying a smoke. "Cam, go fetch Constable Merryweather."

"Why?"

"There's a dead mort in the sacristy."

"Who?"

Oh, for heaven's sakes.

"It doesn't matter who. Just fetch the constable and don't dawdle, mind you."

"Can I take the hearse?"

"Yes, you may."

Cam rushed out, seemingly thrilled to drive the vehicle. To each their own, I supposed. He must have driven at speed, for not twenty minutes later he was back with two police officers in tow who immediately came forward to greet us.

"I'm Constable Merryweather and this is Sergeant Purdy." The constable appeared to be in his early thirties, the sergeant in his forties. "I understand someone discovered the body of a woman in the sacristy."

"My fiancée and I did," Robert answered.

The constable fetched a small notebook and a pencil from the inside of his jacket. "And you would be?"

"Robert Crawford Sinclair, and this is my fiancée, Catherine Worthington." He pointed to his brother. "My brother, Lord Rutledge, and his manservant, Nigel Saybrook.

They did not enter the sacristy, but Miss Worthington and I did."

"Why did you do so?"

"Vicar Mayfield is missing, young man," Lord Rutledge interrupted. "He was supposed to be here to conduct the funeral."

Constable Merryweather glanced around. "He's missing then."

"That's what I just said." Lord Rutledge's patience was starting to wear thin.

"What about Mister Lawson, the curate?"

"Not here either," the undertaker said.

"That's very odd," Sergeant Purdy said.

"Yes, it is," Robert said. "May I suggest you look in the sacristy? The woman needs to be identified."

"Aye," Constable Merryweather said. "And taken to Doctor Springwell. The town physician. He does our post-mortems."

"I can take on that task," the undertaker offered.

"Thank you, Mister Diggum." Once the constable finished taking down the details of our arrival and the reason for our presence, he and the sergeant proceeded to the sacristy. As the last thing we wished was to get involved, we remained where we were.

We waited in various states of impatience for them to return. After fifteen minutes or so, the constable came back by himself.

"Well?" Lord Rutledge asked.

"Freya Poole."

"Ha!" Lord Rutledge said. "That shrew finally got her comeuppance."

"Sir!" Robert said, a warning not to say more. Unfortunately, the constable had picked up on the animosity.

"You knew her."

Lord Rutledge scrunched his mouth. "I met her briefly many years ago. It was not a pleasant experience."

"How so?"

"I'd just discovered I had a brother." Lord Rutledge nodded toward Robert. "She made scurrilous remarks about his mother."

"And when was that?"

Lord Rutledge pondered the question for a few seconds. "I believe it was 1909."

"And you never saw her again?"

His lip curled. "Why would I want to?"

"Right."

"You should have Doctor Springwell examine the body as soon as possible," Robert suggested. More than likely because he was eager to end his brother's interrogation.

Constable Merryweather scrutinized Robert. "My sergeant is attending to it. You seem to be familiar with police procedure."

"I'm a Chief Detective Inspector at Scotland Yard."

"Ahh, well, that explains it." Constable Merryweather paused for a moment before he spoke once more. "The funeral of your mother can't be held today."

Robert rubbed a hand across his brow. "Understandably so."

"I'm sorry. I know how painful it must be."

The constable had a great manner. I had to give him that.

"I suggest you return to Castle Rutledge, but you can't leave. I may have more questions."

Robert pinned a hard gaze on the constable. "We won't be leaving, Sir, until we've buried my mother."

And there it was. What I'd feared. Our time at Castle Rutledge would be longer than we'd planned. But there was no help for it. We had to do what was right.

CHAPTER 8

CONSTABLE INVESTIGATES

The following morning Mister Benton approached Robert with the same lugubrious expression he'd greeted us two days before. "Begging your pardon, Lord Robert, Constable Merryweather would like a word. I explained to him you were only just breaking your fast, but he insists it's important."

"Thank you, Benton," Robert said. "We were just about finished, so no harm done." And then he turned toward me. "Would you like to join us?"

"Yes, of course," I said, after taking a last sip of the excellent coffee.

Benton sniffed. "I showed him to the *small* drawing room."

Of course he had. The constable would not be welcomed in the formal one. That was reserved for family and important guests. In his mind, the local constable did not qualify as either. Well, that was about to change. "Mister Benton, could you see that coffee and tea are brought there, please?"

His brow arched, but all he said was, "Yes, of course, Miss Worthington."

What Mister Benton failed to realize was that we needed to be in the constable's good graces. Snubbing him would benefit no one, least of all Lord Rutledge.

"I hope the constable doesn't wish to speak to your brother." After we returned from the church, he'd retired to his room, and we hadn't seen him since. Not that I was surprised. He'd taken painstaking care to plan the funeral of Robert's mother. Not only had it not taken place, but a dead body had been found at the church. Such circumstances would upset anyone.

Upon entering the small drawing room, Robert greeted the police officer as affably as he greeted anyone. "Good morning, Constable."

"Morning, Sir, err, Lord Robert," the constable said. He appeared somewhat nervous, a contrast to his demeanor at the church. But then the impressive castle was bound to have that effect.

"Please take a seat," I pointed to a very comfortable wing chair. "Coffee and tea should arrive soon."

"Thank you, Miss Worthington. You're very kind."

After Robert and I settled ourselves on the settee across from him, a maid arrived with the tea service. Benton had unbent enough to include a plate of scones that smelled heavenly. I plated two for the good constable along with the tea.

"You have some news?" Robert prompted after giving the constable time to enjoy the refreshments.

"Yes, Sir, er, Lord Robert."

It was going to be a long morning, I could tell.

"I visited the vicar. He overslept. That's why he was not at the church."

"That's unfortunate. Is that a usual occurrence?" I asked. A vicar who misses Sunday service because he's still in bed would not last long.

"No. It's not. First time it's happened as a matter of fact. And the vicar has served our community for a number of years. A very conscientious man of God he is."

"Did he offer an explanation?" Robert asked.

The constable cleared his throat. "He couldn't believe he'd overslept as he normally wakes at seven even when he takes sleeping powders which he did the night before. As the packets had been prescribed by the local apothecary, Mister Sloane, I took them to him to test."

Robert made a noise in his throat, a clear disapproval of the constable's actions. The sleeping powders needed to be tested by someone other than the apothecary who'd prescribed them. But there was nothing that could be done about it now. The harm was done.

"And what did he find?" Robert asked.

"The sleeping packets contained double the dosage he'd prescribed."

"Somebody purposefully altered the dosage then?"

"Not altered, replaced them."

"How did he know?" I asked.

"Mister Sloane stamps all his sleeping packets with his mark. The sleeping packets that were in the vicar's possession did not have it on any of them."

"How many were left?" Robert asked.

"Ten."

"Does the vicar take them every night?"

"No. Only when he can't fall asleep. He knew how important the funeral was, so he wanted a good night's rest. That's why he took the medicine."

"The packets could have been there for days," Robert commented.

"Yes."

"Who has access to the house?"

"Mrs. Reilly, the housekeeper. She also cooks for the vicar."

"Does she live there?"

"No. She has a home of her own. She comes to the vicarage in the morning and leaves after she cleans up after supper." The constable cleared his throat. "There's more, Lord Robert."

"Go on."

"Three days before the funeral was to take place, Lord Rutledge informed the vicar he wanted to inspect the church. They agreed to meet there. The vicar arrived a few minutes late. He'd been counseling a parishioner who'd come to him aggrieved."

"Aggrieved?" I asked.

"The vicar didn't explain. It was a confidential matter."

"Yes, of course."

"He walked into the church to the sounds of an argument. Lord Rutledge and Freya Poole."

Oh, dear. Lord Rutledge had said he met Freya Poole several years ago, but he never mentioned seeing her again.

"What were they arguing about?" Robert asked.

"He doesn't know. They stopped as soon as they saw him. And then Freya Poole stormed out." A pause. "You see how this looks, Sir."

"Yes. Yes, I do." Rather than comment about it, Robert asked. "Do you have any news about the inquest?"

"It will be held tomorrow at The Angry Swan, our local pub. The coroner will notify you about it later today. He'll expect all of you, especially Lord Rutledge, to be in attendance."

"Anything else?"

"No. That's all for now. "I'll see you tomorrow?"

"Yes. We all will be there."

I wrapped the remaining scones in one of the castle napkins and handed them to the constable. Someone was bound to notice the missing cloth. I would need to inform Benton where it'd gone.

"Thank you," the constable said, seemingly pleased.

As busy as he must be, he probably hadn't had a chance to enjoy a full breakfast. The scones would at least keep hunger pains away. "You're most kind to keep us informed, constable."

After he left, I asked Robert, "What do you think?"

"I think my brother is in a world of trouble."

I couldn't help but agree with him.

CHAPTER 9

INQUEST

*T*he Angry Swan was surprisingly spacious for a public house. But then it probably served different purposes, not only did it serve as a place for locals to gather but it served other purposes such as today's inquest and maybe a wedding celebration or two. As one would expect of a public house, there was a bar counter, behind which rows of spirits resided with Rutledge Malt Whisky prominently featured. But behooving the seriousness of the proceedings, no alcohol was being served today. Tables would have occupied a large portion of the space, but they had been removed. Two dozen chairs had been arranged in rows of six to the right of an officious looking gentleman most likely the coroner. Indeed, that proved to be the case. Constable Merryweather informed us he served in that capacity not only for Chipping Bliss but the entire county.

When our party of four arrived, Sergeant Purdy showed

us to the front row seats. The undertaker, his son, and the organist were already there.

The coroner started the proceedings by choosing a jury of twelve, all men, from the citizens who'd been standing around and had them seated in the chairs to his left. Once they had done so, they were sworn in by the sergeant.

With that chore done, the coroner banged the gavel on table that functioned as his desk to gain everyone's attention. They were an obedient lot as they immediately quieted down.

"Given the seriousness of these proceedings," the coroner said, "we will all maintain silence. Our purpose here is to determine how Freya Poole died and if any charges should be brought. I will call witnesses to the stand so they may shed light on the matter. After each person is sworn in, I will question each one before they're dismissed." He glanced at a paper on the desk. "We will start with Constable Merryweather."

After the constable provided his name and occupation, the coroner asked, "Please describe the events of the morning of October 12."

The constable retrieved the small notebook I'd seen before from the inside of his policeman's jacket. "At 24 past 11, Mister Cameron Diggum rushed into the constabulary. He informed me that a woman's body had been found at the church. Both Sergeant Purdy and I accompanied him back to the church. Upon my arrival, I proceeded to the sacristy where I found Freya Poole seated on a chair, dressed in the vicar's vestments. I felt for her pulse. There was none."

"Was there anyone inside the sacristy other than Freya Poole?"

"No, Sir."

"Who else was at the church?"

Again, the constable consulted his notebook. "Lord

Rutledge; his brother, Lord Robert Sinclair; Lord Robert's fiancée, Catherine Worthington; Lord Rutledge's attendant, Nigel Saybrook; the organist, Joe Houghton; the undertaker, Albert Diggum, and his son, Cam Diggum."

"What about the vicar?"

"He wasn't there, Sir."

"Why were these individuals at the church?"

"The remains of Lord Robert's mother were to be laid alongside her husband, the former Marquis Rutledge. She'd been originally buried on the church grounds."

The coroner made a note of that in his notebook. "So what did you do then?"

"I sent Sergeant Purdy to Doctor Springwell's surgery to inform him we needed his services."

"When did everyone arrive at the church?"

The constable referred to his notes. "The organist, Joe Houghton, arrived around ten. He wanted to warm up the organ."

A round of laughter ran through the jury. They must have known Mister Houghton was a heavy drinker.

The coroner banged down the gavel. "Silence."

The room quieted down.

"Go on, Constable."

"The undertaker and his son were the next to arrive. Around fifteen past ten or so. They didn't see the vicar or the curate but did spot the organist. Lord Rutledge's party arrived at the church at thirty past ten. Since the vicar was missing Lord Robert and Miss Worthington went in search of him. That's when they found Freya Poole. Lord Robert then asked the undertaker's son to fetch me, or rather fetch the local policeman."

"What happened then?"

"I allowed the Rutledge party to leave. They didn't need to be there for the rest. At five after twelve, Doctor Springwell arrived. After he declared Freya Poole dead, he asked Mister Diggum to transfer her remains to his surgery so he could perform the postmortem."

"Very well. Is there anything else you'd like to add about the events at the church?"

He cleared his throat. "Not at the moment, Sir."

"Very well. Let's have Doctor Springwell to the stand."

After the doctor had been sworn in, the coroner asked him to verify what the Constable had said. Once that was done, he asked, "Have you performed a postmortem on Freya Poole?"

"I have."

"Do you have a time of death?"

"She died approximately twelve hours before she was found at the church. I would say between ten to midnight the previous day."

The coroner wrote in his notebook.

"Have you determined the cause of death?"

"Yes, Sir. She was poisoned."

A murmur ran through the crowd. The coroner banged down the gavel again. "Silence, please."

"And how did you determine that?"

"I examined the contents of her stomach. She had a supper of beans and toast. That meal had been partly digested before she enjoyed a malted whiskey. In my opinion that's how the poison was delivered as her death would have been almost instantaneous."

"What was the poison?"

"Hemlock."

"Were there any other signs of violence committed against her?"

"Isn't the poison enough?" Doctor Springwell asked. Someone started to laugh, but after a stern glance from the coroner, he soon stopped.

"Please answer the question."

"No. Nothing else."

"Thank you, Doctor Springwell." Once the physician stepped away, the coroner asked, "Let's have the organist, shall we?"

Joseph Houghton had not only sobered up since the last time we saw him but had applied a razor to his face. He'd also taken effort with his clothes. Although not in the height of fashion, they were clean.

"You were at the church the morning of the events surrounding Freya Poole's death?"

"Yes, Sir. I arrived at ten. The undertaker and his son arrived shortly after I did with the remains of Lady Rutledge. Prettiest coffin I've ever seen. All inlaid wood. Gold handles."

"What about the vicar?"

"He wasn't there, which was odd. So I thought I'd enjoy a tipple before the service. It loosens you up wonderfully, it does."

A ripple of laughter ran through the crowd.

The coroner banged down the gavel a third time, and the crowd quieted down. "What did you do while you waited?"

"I took another swallow. Maybe two."

Or maybe the whole bottle. The man had smelled like a brewery.

"Rutledge malt whiskey is the best, don't you know?" The organist asked.

"I don't partake of spirits, Mister Houghton," the coroner said with a frown.

"You're missing out, your worship."

The coroner let out a heavy sigh. "What happened next?"

"Well, I saw his lordship and his family arrive, so I went to introduce myself. Unfortunately, I tripped and fell. Cam Diggum helped me to a pew."

"Yyou saw the undertaker and his son arrive, as well as Lord Rutledge and his party?"

"Yes, Sir."

"Did you see anyone else?"

"No."

After Joseph Houghton, we were all called to the stand. First Lord Rutledge, then his attendant, followed by Robert and me. We all verified what the constable had said.

The coroner then called the vicar to the stand. A dignified-looking gentleman, in his early fifties going by the grey in his hair.

"You were to be present for the funeral?"

"I was." His voice was deep and resonant, just as a vicar's should be.

"Why weren't you?"

"I took sleeping powders the night before. I would have awakened in plenty of time to attend the service. Unfortunately, I overslept." He glanced at Lord Rutledge. "I apologize, Your Lordship. If I had known, I would have never—"

The coroner interrupted him. "Please direct your comments to me and me only."

"Yes, Sir."

"Do you know why your overslept?"

"Constable Merryweather took the sleeping packets to Mister Sloane, the apothecary who prescribed them. It turns out some contained twice the usual dosage."

The coroner's brow shot up. "Is Mister Sloane on the premises?"

The apothecary stood up. "Yes, Sir."

The coroner dismissed the vicar and swore in the apothecary. Sandy haired and spectacled, he was of average height and built for a man and appeared to be in his early forties. "Did you examine the sleeping packets?"

"Yes, Sir. The one the vicar took was not one of mine. I

never make those sorts of mistakes." He preened. "I take pride in my work."

"How do you know it wasn't one of yours?"

"I mark my packets with my stamp." He retrieved a small wooden stamp with a rubber tip at the end. "This is what I use so it can be known as mine. I had it especially made."

"What did you discover about the sleeping packets?"

"They contained twice the dosage I normally give to the vicar. Should have been fifteen grains of Veronal, but it had thirty. It would have put him deep into sleep for at least twelve hours. No wonder he overslept. Not only that, the packets themselves were not the same papers I use. They were cheap substitutions."

"Very well."

After the apothecary's testimony, the verdict was rendered swiftly by the jury. Murder by person or persons unknown. The constable was charged with the investigation into Freya Poole's murder.

CHAPTER 10

A REQUEST IS MADE

*A*fter the inquest, the drive to Castle Rutledge was mostly conducted in silence as we all had quite a bit to mull over. Luncheon had been arranged for us. But before it could be served, Lord Rutledge declared he was not hungry and begged to be excused.

That did not sit right with Robert. "I'm afraid that will not do, Sir." Given Lord Rutledge's frail health, the last thing he should do was stop eating.

With a curl to his lip, Lord Rutledge turned back to him. "I beg your pardon."

"You've already missed one meal today." We hadn't seen Lord Rutledge at breakfast. "You must eat to keep up your strength."

"Who exactly is the lord of this castle?"

Oh, dear.

"You are. But this has nothing to do with your status. It has to do with your well-being."

"If you must know, I had breakfast in my chambers."

Robert sniffed. "I don't believe you."

Lord Rutledge's face turned a mottled shade of red. "Why, you insolent puppy!"

He'd never addressed Robert in such a manner before. But then these were trying circumstances. I had to step in before they both blurted out something they would regret. "Lord Rutledge, may I say something?"

He waved a hand toward me, which I took as approval.

"Robert and I care very much about you. The current circumstances are very troubling indeed. But it's something we need to face together. And that can't happen if you keep to your rooms." I glanced at Robert who nodded. "Won't you please join us for lunch?"

Lord Rutledge scrunched his mouth while he weighed my suggestion. Reaching a conclusion, he said, "I don't want to discuss anything unpleasant during the meal. It upsets my digestion."

I offered him my brightest smile. "Then we won't." I curled my hand around his elbow and together we strolled toward the drawing room where the meal would be served while Robert trailed us. Thankfully, Benton had made it nice and cozy with the fireplace blazing with heat, a good thing for the day had turned cold and blustery.

Once Lord Rutledge settled himself at the head of the table, Robert and I took the seats on either side of him.

Benton wasted no time serving the first course. The pearl barley soup, accompanied by slices of rosemary bread, was truly delicious. Lord Rutledge must have thought the same as he ate every drop.

Once the meat dish was served, I guided the conversation toward a topic that had sparked my curiosity. "I didn't know you brewed your own single malt whiskey. How did that come to be?"

"It's been in the family for ages," Lord Rutledge explained. "Since the fifteenth century, as a matter of fact when one of my ancestors realized the benefit of growing barley. Not only did it serve as food, such as the soup we just enjoyed, but it could be used to brew single malt whiskey."

"How very clever of your ancestor," I said.

"Yes, it was rather. At first, we brewed it only for the castle residents. But as word got around, we got a demand for it from the local public house and residents of the village. It didn't stop there, however. In those days Chipping Bliss was a market town which meant people would come for miles around to sell and buy goods. They often stopped at the public house for food and drink, including our whiskey. Soon we started getting orders from nearby towns and eventually cities."

"That's truly fascinating. Isn't it, Robert?" He'd been eating silently the entire meal. No doubt troubled by what we'd learned at the inquest.

"It is." A terse reply, with every ounce of emotion missing from it.

Lord Rutledge's brow arched. "You'll need to familiarize yourself with the running of the brewery, Robert. You should do that while you're here for one day you'll inherit the lot." Even though it'd been voiced as a directive, Lord Rutledge's tone was laced with fondness.

"Indeed, Sir." Another polite response. Clearly Robert's thoughts were somewhere else. Was he ruminating over the events of the day? Or did his lack of interest spring from something more serious? The assumption of the title meant responsibility for everything that went along with it, which meant not only Castle Rutledge but the brewery as well. Was that responsibility weighing on his mind? It was something I would need to explore. I'd have to tread carefully, though. Emotionally, he was operating on a razor's edge.

The rest of the meal passed pleasantly enough with Lord Rutledge and me carrying the conversation while Robert contributed brief replies. When finished, Lord Rutledge announced he was retiring to his rooms for the afternoon to rest.

"I trust that meets with your approval, my dear?" He asked me. "These old bones aren't what they used to be."

"Of course, Sir. Not that you need my approval."

He got a hold of my hand, brought it to his lips, and kissed it. "I'm so glad you'll be marrying Robert. You will make a fine lady of the castle someday."

The highest compliment indeed. "Not for a long time, I hope. But I thank you. Enjoy your rest, Your Lordship."

From seemingly out of nowhere, his attendant appeared. While he did not help Lord Rutledge ascend the stairs, he followed along to offer whatever assistance was needed.

Robert and I were enjoying our coffee when Benton stepped into the drawing room. "Constable Merryweather wishes a word, Lord Robert. I've shown him to the small drawing room and arranged for refreshments."

Obviously, Mister Benton learned well.

"Yes, of course." Robert slowly folded his napkin, placed it on the table, and came to his feet.

After I'd done the same, we headed toward the drawing room. "You were expecting him, weren't you?" I asked.

"Yes, I was."

"That's what kept your mind busy during the luncheon?"

He nodded.

When we entered the room, we found Constable Merryweather standing once more. Unlike his previous visit, he refused the seat we offered. When the maid entered with the coffee service, he also refused it. That did not portend well.

"What can we do for you, Constable?" Robert asked.

"I'm afraid we've discovered something rather alarming."

Of course he had.

"I found a bottle of Castle Rutledge Malt Whiskey in Freya Poole's front room, right next to the chair she used in the evenings. Both the glass she drank from and the bottle contained hemlock, the poison the doctor found in her stomach. If you'll recall his testimony, she would have died a short time after ingesting the whiskey."

"Why didn't you report that at the inquest?"

"I sent the bottle to a chemist to have it tested. I did not get back the results until after the inquest concluded."

"Castle Rutledge Malt Whiskey is sold in the village," Robert pointed out. "Anyone could have brought the bottle to her."

"Indeed. However, this bottle was labeled Rutledge Malt Whiskey Special Reserve. That recipe is exclusively brewed for the castle. The only bottles to be found are right here."

"Or at the brewery," Robert said. "Someone from either the castle or the brewery could have given it to her. You'll have to trace it, of course. Did you dust the bottle for fingermarks?"

Constable Merryweather's face tinged a shade of pink. "No, Sir. I'm afraid we don't have the ability to do so."

More than likely, the sleepy village of Chipping Bliss had had no prior need for one.

"You'll need a forensics kit then. Shall I telephone Scotland Yard and have them rush you one?"

"Thank you. I appreciate the kindness."

"You should have one on hand," Robert said waving away the gratitude. "Have you confiscated the bottle?"

Constable Merryweather nodded. "I've secured it in evidence."

"Wearing gloves, I hope?"

"Yes, Sir. However, my sergeant was not as careful. He was the one who found it."

"A shame, that."

The constable cleared his throat. "Lord Robert, we've had a small number of deaths in the village since I became its constable two years ago, most of which stemmed from natural causes or accidents. The only one that was deemed manslaughter was a fight that broke out in the pub over a lady. And that was easily solved as there were several witnesses. But, as you can see, this murder investigation is beyond me. I need help."

Robert folded his hands along his back. "Indeed you do, Constable. Have you requested it of Scotland Yard? They might be able to assign someone."

"I was hoping that would be you, Lord Robert."

Robert's brow arched upward. "Do you think that would be appropriate? I'm Lord Rutledge's brother. The bottle alone points to the castle."

"Maybe not, but a stranger would not be welcomed by the villagers. They're a close lot."

"I'm a stranger," Robert said.

"But you're the heir to the title, and one day you will inherit the castle, live among them. They're more likely to trust you than someone else. And more than that, I've followed your career at Scotland Yard. You have a reputation for honesty and trustworthiness."

"If the evidence pointed away from my brother, those qualities might very well be questioned."

"I know things look rather grim for Lord Rutledge. But he's in a rather frail state if you don't mind my saying so. He wouldn't have been able to carry Miss Poole to the church."

"He could have hired someone," Robert said.

"True. His manservant is a strapping young man. We'll need to interrogate him, of course. But my instincts tell me Lord Rutledge is not guilty of the crime."

Clearly, the constable's mind was made up. He wanted Lord Robert and no one else to help with the investigation.

Robert apparently had reached the same conclusion. "I'll need to discuss this with my brother. You'll have my·answer in the morning."

"I'll await your message, Sir." Having delivered his request, Constable Merryweather took his leave.

"What are you thinking?" I asked Robert once we were alone.

He brushed a hand across his troubled brow. "It's a damnable thing."

"Yes, it is." The reinterment of his birth mother's remains was stressful enough. And now his beloved brother was a likely murder suspect, no matter what Constable Merryweather said. Robert was more than capable of dealing with just about anything. But this investigation would most certainly tax his endurance to the limit. I reached out for his hand and held it in mine. It was so very cold. "Are you considering taking this on?"

"It depends."

I knew what he was thinking. Before he took on this investigation, he would need to discover what Lord Rutledge's argument with Freya Poole had been about.

CHAPTER 11

THE INVESTIGATION BEGINS

*A*s Lord Rutledge kept to his chambers the rest of the day, Robert had to wait until he joined us for supper to discuss the matter with him. Thankfully, he was in a chipper mood than he'd seemed before. The rest had done him a world of good.

Robert didn't broach the subject until we moved to the small drawing room to enjoy our post meal coffee and cordials. It being late in the evening, the temperature had dropped, but the fireplace was blazing away lending warmth and an air of coziness to the room.

Robert didn't waste time bringing up the topic foremost in his mind. "We had a visit from Constable Merryweather."

"What did he have to say?" Lord Rutledge asked.

Robert related what the policeman had asked of him.

Lord Rutledge didn't immediately react. He took a sip of his coffee before he did. "Are you thinking of taking this on?"

"It depends, Sir."

"On what?"

"On what your argument with Freya Poole was about."

Lord Rutledge's cup landed on the saucer with a clatter, some of the liquid spilling over. "It had nothing to do with her murder."

"Maybe so. Still, I need to know." Robert was standing his ground. "I can't conduct this investigation without knowing what I'm walking into."

Lord Rutledge's mouth worked with emotion before he spoke up. "She questioned your legitimacy."

I hitched a breath.

"How?" Robert asked.

"She claimed the marriage certificate was a fake. That I falsified it when I discovered you'd been born. She said she had proof."

"Did you in fact create a fake certificate?"

"Of course not!" Lord Rutledge exclaimed. "The very idea that I would do such a thing."

"What proof did she have?"

"The church where Father married your mother burned down taking the parish records with it."

"But they would have been filed with the registry office in London."

"Yes, I know." Lord Rutledge sounded less sure at this point.

"Were they in fact filed, Sir?"

Lord Rutledge pounded the arm of his chair. "I don't know, blast it. I never checked. There was no need to do so. We had the marriage certificate. That was enough for the Chancery Court to declare you my legal heir."

"I'm sure it's a tempest in a teacup, Lord Rutledge," I said trying to cool the heated discourse. "We can easily check those records."

"Not through Scotland Yard!" He demanded. "I don't want them getting involved in this matter."

"No, of course not," I said. "I'll telephone my brother Ned in the morning and ask him to look into it."

"Yes, that would work." He came to his feet and, just like the night before, his attendant appeared like magic. "Now I'm going to bed. I've had enough excitement for the day."

Robert stood as well. "Yes, of course, Sir. Sleep well." Once Lord Rutledge was no longer within hearing distance, Robert said, "He's afraid."

"Yes. Of what we may find."

Robert blew out a harsh breath. "Or what we don't."

"Do you think he would have falsified the record?" I asked.

He worried a hand across his jaw. "I don't know. Supposedly, the man of business your father recommended found the marriage certificate."

"That was about twelve years ago?"

"More like fourteen."

"Is he still employed by Lord Rutledge?"

"Oh, yes. I met him in London. Very capable individual."

"Father wouldn't have recommended him otherwise. We'll need to talk to him as well."

He turned back to me. "We?"

"Yes, we. I'm helping. We'll need to get others involved as well. We can't be going back and forth to London when the murder investigation is conducted here. Ned would be the best one to get all the details. The business manager worked at Worthington & Son so Ned would know him. I'll ask him to check the registry records as well."

"Your brother is a busy man. Will he drop everything to do this?"

I gazed at him in wonder. "Of course he will. We're family."

He took my hand and gently pulled me into him. "Have I told you how much I love you?"

"Not recently, no."

"Well, then, let me remedy that." A kiss was all it took to convince me once more of his love.

We spent the next thirty minutes or so discussing how to proceed with the investigation. In the morning, we would put them into action. Satisfied with our tentative plans, we made our way to our respective rooms.

Just as we were approaching my door, an alarming thought occurred to me. "Oh, dear!"

"What's wrong?"

"Mother is expecting us back in London tomorrow. She needs to learn what has occurred."

"I'll leave that to you then, shall I?" He said with a nonchalant air which didn't fool me one bit.

"Coward!" I teased him.

"Prudent," he countered. "I'm marrying her daughter, so I'd just as soon stay in her good graces."

"Umm," was all I said as I slipped into my room.

CHAPTER 12

THE VICAR AND HIS HOUSEKEEPER

*A*fter breakfast the following morning I put in a trunk call to Mother. When she heard my news, she was upset. Predictably so. But she understood the necessity of us remaining at Castle Rutledge until the investigation concluded.

"What about your pre-wedding festivities?" She'd organized a tea with a select group of ladies from the upper strata of society after she'd determined a future marchioness needed to make her mark in their world. As busy as I had been with the Ladies of Distinction Detective Agency, it was something I'd largely ignored.

"Will you return in time to attend the tea?" Mother asked.

Maybe. Maybe not. I had no idea how long the investigation would take. But I didn't want to squash her hopes and dreams. "We'll do our very best, Mother. I promise."

After I ended the call, I telephoned my brother Ned and made the requests I'd discussed with Robert the night before.

Once I was done, I headed toward the small drawing room where he was waiting for me.

I found him seated at the writing desk jotting something on what I knew to be one of his investigative notebooks. He never traveled anywhere without one.

Glancing up, he asked, "How did your mother take the news?"

"As well as could be expected. She sends you and Lord Rutledge her love."

"We'll need it. Ready to head out?" First thing this morning, he'd telephoned Constable Merryweather to inform him he would assist with the investigation. They'd made plans to visit the vicar at ten. As Robert wished to talk not only with the vicar but the housekeeper as well, he'd asked me to join them. He felt a woman would respond better if another female was present.

I nodded.

Soon we were ensconced in Lord Rutledge's Rolls Royce with his chauffeur at the wheel and me bundled into the coat I'd brought with me. It'd turned downright frosty overnight.

"I wish we'd brought your automobile," I said. "This one is a bit too ostentatious for the village." Most of the villagers were folks of modest means. The last thing we should be doing was flashing our wealth. But there was no help for it. The Rolls was the only proper motorcar at Castle Rutledge. The other modes of transportation were a truck of dubious origin, bicycles, and horse drawn carts.

"We didn't know we'd be involved in a murder investigation. We'll just have to make the best of it."

The vicar had been expecting us. Tall, distinguished looking, his dark hair peppered with gray, he was exactly what one expected a vicar to be. After warmly welcoming us, he led the way to the front room.

No sooner were we seated than the housekeeper, Mrs.

Reilly, bustled in with the tea service. It consisted of a fragrant Earl Grey and scrumptious scones, freshly baked for our visit. After settling the tray on a round table, she departed, gently closing the door behind her.

The vicar's answers pretty much matched what Constable Merryweather had revealed the day before, and, of course, the testimony the vicar had given at the inquest. Still, Robert had more questions. "Someone entered the church, more than likely in the dark of night. It was not broken into as far as I noticed. I found that rather odd."

The vicar offered a soft smile. "I believe the house of God should be available to anyone who seeks spiritual comfort no matter the time of day. The church is always open. So is the vicarage for that matter."

A marked difference from London houses of worship which were locked up tight from evening until morning. City thieves would make off with anything that wasn't nailed down. And sometimes that as well.

"You're not afraid someone will steal your valuables?" Robert asked.

"They're locked up in a secure place known only to me and my curate."

I glanced around. "Is he here?"

"He's away at the moment. His mother has grown quite ill. That's one of the reasons I was so worried about the funeral arrangements. I depended on him to manage some of the details. But with him gone, I had to attend to all of them myself." A rueful smile bloomed across his mouth. "I'm not the best with the lesser particulars."

"When did he leave?" Robert asked.

"Two days before the funeral was to take place."

After noting the vicar's answers in his notebook, Robert said, "I'd like to turn now to Freya Poole."

A frown replaced the vicar's affable grin. "A less than amiable woman, I'm sorry to say."

"In what way?" Robert asked.

"She loved to cause discord among the villagers. She thrived on it."

"How did she do that?" I asked.

"By spreading malicious tales. Hardly a family was unaffected by it. Needless to say, she was strongly disliked."

"Anyone in particular?"

The vicar shook his head. "I don't keep track of the village gossip, not the specifics anyway."

As Robert had no more questions of the vicar, at least for the moment, he asked if we could talk with Mrs. Reilly.

"Of course," the vicar said.

When the same request was made of her, Mrs. Reilly readily agreed. Robert and I had discussed her interview the night before and decided to talk to her in the vicarage kitchen. We hoped the familiar setting would lend a measure of comfort to her.

"Thank you for talking to us," I said. Robert and I had agreed I would take the lead on her questioning.

"Ta, dear. Whatever I can do to help."

"How long have you worked for Vicar Mayfield?" Even though I already knew the answer, I wanted to ease into the conversation with a question that would hopefully put her at ease.

"Since he arrived several years ago. He's a very nice gentleman. No fuss keeps himself to himself. It's a pleasure to do for him and Mister Lawson as well."

"Mister Lawson lives here?"

"Oh, yes, indeed, dearie. There's more than enough space. Two bedrooms upstairs. And on this floor, the front room, the study, and the kitchen. Both partake of their meals right here every morning, noon, and evening."

"And you like cooking for them." A statement, not a question. I could clearly see how much pride she took in her cooking.

"Indeed, I do. They both enjoy hearty appetites."

"That's wonderful. Now, Mrs. Reilly I'd like to ask you about the time before the funeral. Did the vicar receive any visitors in the days before?"

She gazed off into the distance. "Now, let me see. The vicar had a pre-wedding consultation with Jenny Marsh and Rob Nettles. Such a nice couple. They're well-matched."

I shared a loving look with Robert.

"Much as the two of you are," Mrs. Reilly said. "If you will indulge me for a moment, Lord Robert."

"Yes, of course."

"I knew your mother, Susan. A lovely lass she was."

Robert froze. No wonder. It was the first time he'd heard anyone who knew her speak about his mother.

Eager to encourage Mrs. Reilly' recollections, I asked. "Was she?"

"Yes, indeed. She came to Chipping Bliss when she was in her mid-twenties. Her da had passed away, you see. Having nowhere else to live she came to her aunt, Flora. Poor thing. She was doing poorly herself. Susan was a saint the way she cared for her. It was the happiest I ever saw Flora. But there was no improving her lot and she passed three years later. She left the cottage to Susan, and a bit of money as well. Susan didn't have to work or marry. Still, she kept herself busy gardening and such. She made that cottage a showplace. She was a dab hand at sewing and embroidering as well. Made herself a wedding gown and veil. To dream on, she said. She was twenty-nine by then and didn't expect to marry."

I swallowed hard. "And the marquis?"

"Big, brawny man. Kind. Not a bit of the toff about him.

You're the spitting image of him, Lord Robert, if you don't mind my saying so."

"So I've been told." Robert grinned, and Mrs. Reilly sighed softly. Not the first time I'd seen him have that effect on women.

"Now and again, he would drop by The Angry Swan and have a drink with the lads. During harvest season, he'd buy rounds for the entire house."

"How did he meet Susan?" I asked.

"In church. He attended whenever he was at the castle. Not every Sunday mind you, but often enough. After her aunt passed, she became involved in more of the social activities there. It was at the rumble sale when they first set eyes on each other. It was like they were both struck by lightning it was. Mind you, he was a bit older than her."

I'd say. She was in her late twenties, and he was in his late forties.

"He came into the village more often then, no doubt hoping to catch sight of her. She tried to avoid him. He's quality, she'd say, when I brought up His Lordship. But I had eyes in me head, didn't I? I could tell they were sweet on each other. That year for Christmas, he invited the whole village to the castle. Gave presents to all the children. Food, music, dancing. It was glorious. When the two of them danced, it was plain as the nose on me face they were in love."

"What happened after that?"

"He visited her cottage. Oh, he'd try to hide it. Stabled his mount in a shed behind the house. But the whole town knew. And then that spring, she was with child. She was so happy. Of course, there were those in the village who started calling her names, especially Freya Poole. A mean old biddy she was. But most of the village didn't care a fig." She swallowed hard. "And then that summer the marquis passed away suddenly. She was devastated. Couldn't stop crying. It was like the light had gone out of her. He'll never see his child, she said. There was no consoling her." She breathed out a hard sigh. "She went into labor that fall. The midwife, she was the best she was. She tried everything to save her. But Susan had given up. The child died with her, or so the midwife claimed."

"Only he didn't," I said. "The babe lived."

Mrs. Reilly reached out to pat Robert's hand. "And thank God he did."

CHAPTER 13

THE PHYSICIAN

*A*fter leaving the vicarage, we were to meet with Doctor Springwell to discuss the postmortem. But after the emotional conversation with Mrs. Reilly, I questioned the wisdom of conducting that interview at this time. The revelations about Robert's mother had taken a toll on him. Not that he'd let on. Still, I had to make the suggestion. "Maybe we should postpone the visit until tomorrow."

"He might not be available then, Catherine," Robert answered in his even-keeled manner, "and he's already expecting us. It would be best to proceed as planned."

"Very well. If that's what you wish."

"It is." I could see there was no dissuading him.

As the doctor was located on the opposite end of the village from the vicarage, we made our way there in the Rolls Royce. Along the way, we passed The Angry Swan where several men were standing outside. Most watched in silence as we drove by, but one spat on the ground.

"Who was that?" I asked the constable.

"Bill Poole. Don't pay him no mind. He's a scofflaw and a drunkard. Constantly in trouble. He's spent more time in gaol than out."

"Poole? Is he related to Freya Poole?"

"Her brother. No love lost between them. She tossed him out of her cottage years ago."

"Given the enmity between them, he could be a suspect."

"Possibly. We'd need to determine how he obtained a bottle of the malt whiskey, though."

"That's true for anyone we identify as a suspect," Robert said.

The constable nodded. "You're right. But it'd be especially difficult for him. He never has any coin."

"Was Freya Poole a drinker?" I asked.

"She enjoyed her tipple, although never to excess like her brother. It was a nightly ritual with her."

Which meant her brother would have most certainly known.

Doctor Springwell was indeed expecting us. Thankfully, the body was not there. So I didn't have to witness that. One look at her mottled blue face had been enough for me. Although Doctor Springwell provided extensive documentation of the chemist's findings, he added no more information. Freya Poole had been poisoned by the hemlock that had been poured into the malt whiskey.

"Could it have been introduced another way?" Robert asked. "A cup of tea maybe?"

"I don't see how. Hemlock has a bitter taste. It would have been masked by the malt whiskey but certainly not by any tea I know."

Constable Merryweather cleared his throat. "We didn't find any other food or drink in her cottage which would account for the poison. Her normal routine was to enjoy her supper and then at some point sit in her chair by the fireplace to enjoy her nightly drink."

"She preferred single malt whiskey?" Robert asked the constable.

"Yes. She'd buy a bottle from the public house."

"Could she have obtained this particular bottle herself?"

"No. Not this one. It was the wrong vintage."

"What do you mean?" I asked.

"The bottles used by the public house are from this year's vintage or at most the year before. This one was brewed in 1919."

"So somebody bought it at that time?" I asked.

"Or been awarded it," the doctor added.

"Awarded? How?" Robert asked.

"At the end of harvest season, the Castle Rutledge estate manager holds a harvest celebration," the doctor explained. "Games and such. The winner of the foot race is rewarded with a bottle of the Castle Rutledge Special Reserve."

"How long has this been going on?" Robert asked.

"Since the flood," the constable answered.

"How many winners?"

"Who are still alive? I don't know maybe twenty men."

"No women?" I asked.

The constable shook his head. "Ladies are not allowed to enter the foot race."

Figures!

"The celebration was not held during the time of the Great War," the constable continued. "But it resumed the year after."

"Who won the race that year?" Robert asked.

"Let me see," the doctor said. "Mister Lawson, I believe."

"The curate?"

The good doctor nodded. "Doubt he still has it. It's been five years."

"We'll need to ask him when he returns," I suggested.

"Or we can search his room at the vicarage," Robert said. Turning back to the doctor, he asked, "Did you find any marks of violence on Freya Poole?"

I hadn't seen any. But then, after one glance, I'd looked away.

"Only the ones you'd expect to find when a body has been dragged," the doctor explained. "There were marks on her wrists. I imagine the person grabbed her by them and tossed her over his shoulder. And then in the dark of night he would have made his way to the church."

CHAPTER 14

BACK AT CASTLE RUTLEDGE

*B*y the time we were done with the physician, it was nearly one in the afternoon. Feeling a bit peckish, I asked Constable Merryweather, "Does The Angry Swan serve food?"

"Bangers and Mash, Pasties. Not your usual fare, I would expect."

"We're not so high in our instep, Constable. Robert and I quite adore pub food." Turning to Robert, I suggested we enjoy our luncheon there. It would provide us with the opportunity to meet more of the locals.

Robert took a moment before he answered, "We should wait until after we've talked to the apothecary to acquaint ourselves with more of the villagers. At that point, we'll have a clearer idea of the facts surrounding the murder."

He had a point. "Whatever you think is best."

"I've scheduled that interview for tomorrow," Constable Merryweather said. "He was not available today."

"We'll head back to Castle Rutledge then," Robert said. "Unless you've arranged something else, Constable?"

"I have not."

"The castle it is then," I said, curling a hand around Robert's elbow before addressing the constable. "Would you care to join us for luncheon there?"

He shook his head. "I'll have to decline. I have matters that need attending at the constabulary. Police work doesn't stop because there's been a murder."

A rueful smile flitted across Robert's mouth. "I know how accurate that is. The paperwork alone can be daunting."

"Too true." The constable cleared his throat. "I need to interview Lord Rutledge. Could you arrange it? Tomorrow would be best. We'll be meeting with the apothecary in the morning at ten."

Robert nodded. Not a surprise. He'd been expecting the request. "I'll have to let you know whether that works with his schedule." And with that he and I slipped into the Rolls.

I knew better than to discuss the investigation with the chauffeur at the wheel, so we turned our conversation to the village. Most of the cottages, built from Cotswold stone, appeared to be at least two hundred years old. It being October, there was little in the way of blossoming foliage. But I could well imagine the beauty of the gardens come spring.

Upon our arrival at the castle, Mister Benton informed us Robert's brother had already enjoyed his luncheon. He was now resting but would like Robert to join him in his study at three. His estate manager wanted to inform Lord Rutledge as to certain matters. It went unsaid that as the heir Robert should be kept apprised of them as well.

"Of course," Robert readily agreed. "Could you get word to him?"

"I will handle it personally, Lord Robert." Mister Benton snapped his fingers, and a footman approached with a salver on which an envelope lay. "A telegram arrived for you, Miss Worthington."

"Oh?" My heart sank. Hoping it wasn't bad news about Dickie, I tore open the envelope in a rush. Reading it both eased and flummoxed me.

"What is it, darling?" Robert asked in a kind voice.

"It's from Ned." I read it to him, *Hollingsworth and I arriving at Moreton on Marsh on the four o'clock train. Items of importance to discuss. Have car meet us at the station. Dickie recuperating nicely.*

"Good to know Richard is healing," Robert said.

I glanced up at him. "Yes, but what could be so important both Ned and Hollingsworth need to travel here?"

"We'll know soon enough." Turning to the butler, he said. "Could you ask Mrs. Collins to make two rooms ready for the gentlemen?"

"Of course, Lord Robert." Another small bow of his head. But this time he included a smile.

He hadn't turned a hair about the rooms, but the housekeeper might have another reaction altogether. Upon my arrival, I'd discovered my sleeping chamber not only spotless, but every gleaming surface polished to a shine. But then the housekeeper had had two days' notice of my visit. As it was now two o'clock, she would have a bare three hours to prepare rooms that might or might not be fit for habitation.

"Would you like your luncheon served in the large drawing room, milord?" The butler asked.

"Yes, that would be fine."

"I'll inform Cook." And with that he strolled away in a somewhat lighter gait. Was it my imagination or was Mister Benton thawing? He no longer appeared the stern butler we'd first met. I supposed time would tell.

It took no time for the meal to be served. A good thing for we were both starving. While we were enjoying the hearty beef stew and the fragrant rolls, Robert and I discussed Ned and Hollingsworth's pending arrival. "I'll go to the rail station to greet them." It seemed churlish not to have one of us meet them there.

After spearing a beef tidbit, Robert said, "Please offer my apologies for not coming as well."

"They'll understand once I tell them about your meeting." Tasting the Cabernet Sauvignon I reveled in the dark fruity aroma infused with spices. One could not fault the Castle Rutledge steward. He kept an excellent wine cellar.

After enjoying his own sip, Robert glanced out the window. "Make sure you take rugs and umbrellas with you. Those dark clouds portend rain."

Not only was the wind rising, but the weather seemed to be turning. "Will do. I'll change into my country clothes as well."

His gaze bounced back to me. "Country clothes?"

I responded with a smile. "A tweed jacket, wool jumper, and trousers. And leather boots, of course."

His mouth quirked. "Not the sort of thing you usually wear in London."

"No." My usual wardrobe consisted of day dresses, business suits, and evening frocks. "As soon as you told me about our trip, I telephoned my modiste with an urgent call for help. The next day she delivered a complete set of country togs. In the latest style, of course." I grinned.

He reached out to squeeze my hand. "You are a wonder, Catherine."

"Oh, I can't take the credit. Angelique is the true wonder." She'd been designing my clothes since my debut last year. And had done a marvelous job.

"What was your opinion of the vicar?" Robert asked once he'd sent the butler and the footmen away. We needed to discuss the investigation in private.

"He's holding something back."

"Yes, I got the same feeling. Any ideas what it could be?"

"He mentioned Freya Poole spreading malicious gossip in the village. I must wonder if some was aimed at him."

"I thought the same thing."

"And yet, you did not ask him about it." A true observation.

"Doubt he would have given an honest answer. We'll find out soon enough. In a village as small as Chipping Bliss, others will have heard any rumors, whatever they are."

"And you think they will share them with you?"

He grinned. "Oh, they'll share the gossip fast enough. They won't be able to help themselves. I'm a Scotland Yard Detective Chief Inspector, after all."

"Whereas us lesser creatures have to resort to other means to discover the truth," I joked.

"I've seen your methods, Miss Worthington. They put mine to shame. Furthermore, you have never, or will ever be, a lesser creature."

"Flattery will get you . . . whatever you want, Inspector." I accompanied this outrageous statement by batting my eyelashes. But suddenly recalling Mother's words, I grew serious.

Which of course Robert noticed. "What's wrong?"

"Nothing." I couldn't very well share Mother's advice with him.

"Now you're the one hiding something."

"It's something Mother said. I'd just as soon not talk about it, if you please."

"Very well."

"I'm ready for dessert. How about you?" I asked more to change the subject than anything else.

"I'll ring for the butler, shall I?" With that he came to his feet and approached the bellpull.

Mister Benton entered within the next few seconds. Clearly, he'd been waiting to be summoned.

"We're done with our meal, Benton. Could you please bring dessert and coffee?"

"Of course, Lord Robert."

The trifle was delicious, and we readily lapped it up. But the meal had grown strained, and we never regained the easy give and take we'd shared earlier.

CHAPTER 15

ALARMING NEWS

*T*he London train was only fifteen minutes late, so I did not have long to wait for my brother and Hollingsworth to arrive. But they were not the only ones. An additional passenger had joined them.

Of course, my priority was to greet Ned and Hollingsworth, but once I'd done that, I addressed the third person. "Mister Hudson, how pleasant to see you." Robert's valet here in the flesh.

"My apologies, Miss Worthington. I should have sent word. But after learning Lord Robert would be staying more than a few days, I felt compelled to pack additional clothes and bring them to his lordship."

"That's very diligent of you." A perfectionist by nature, Mister Hudson couldn't abide the notion of Robert going about in less than his best. "I'm sure Robert will appreciate them and you."

"Thank you."

"Mother also packed additional clothes for you," Ned was not slow to add.

Of course, she did. Mister Hudson was not the only one who worried about wardrobe. Even in a village as small as Chipping Bliss, Mother believed I had to look my best.

As we approached the Rolls Royce with the mountain of luggage, I asked Ned, "How's Dickie?"

He hesitated for a moment before he spoke. "Recuperating nicely. He's now allowed to be up and about most of the day, with only a couple of hours rest."

"That's good. But I sense there's something else."

"He intends to return to Egypt once he's regained his health."

"Oh, dear." It wasn't entirely unexpected. He'd hinted at that resolve when I held that late night conversation with him. After we climbed into the automobile—Ned, Hollingsworth, and I in the back, and Hudson in front—I said, "Mother and Father can't be happy about that."

"They're not. But for the moment they're not disallowing him of that notion. Once he's back on his feet, I expect they'll have something to say."

"I don't see how they can stop him. He has his own money which means he can live in Egypt without any financial help from them." Once us siblings turned twenty-one years of age, Father had settled a quite generous sum on each of us. He wanted his sons and daughters to be able to choose how they lived without fear of poverty.

"Father is arranging something for him in London."

"Mother mentioned it, but she didn't know what he had in mind."

"Neither do I. He's keeping closemouthed about it."

I blew out a breath. "We'll just have to wait then."

"Just so."

Turning to Hollingsworth, I asked. "How are you feeling?" During our previous investigation, he'd been seriously hurt.

He tossed me his irrepressible grin. "Fit as a fiddle, Kitty."

I raised a questioning brow.

He lost the smile. "Well, if you must know, I can't raise my arm above my head, but other than that—"

"You're fit as a fiddle," I said. Unfortunately, that inability could be a disaster for him. He was a seaman. He'd need a functioning arm before he went sailing again. "How long until it heals?"

He shrugged as the corners of his mouth turned down. "Six months? A year? Who knows?"

Lord Newcastle, a mutual friend, had been similarly injured during the Great War. He'd never regained full use of his arm. Curling my hand around his elbow, I said, "I'm sure it will happen sooner than that. You're young, strong."

"Don't forget handsome," he said flashing his cheeky grin once more.

Clearly, he wanted the subject dropped, so I obliged him. As we couldn't very well discuss what had brought them to Castle Rutledge within the listening distance of the chauffeur, I settled on providing a running commentary of Chipping Bliss and Castle Rutledge. If either Ned or Hollingsworth, or both, decided on a longer stay, they would know what to expect.

We arrived at Castle Rutledge to find both Robert and Lord Rutledge waiting for us. After Ned and Hollingsworth were warmly greeted, and Hudson explained his purpose, their bags were taken to their rooms by several footmen with Hudson trailing behind.

As we settled in the formal drawing room for drinks and refreshments, Lord Rutledge asked, "So what brought you to Castle Rutledge, young men? Not that you're not welcome."

"Well, Sir," Ned replied, "Kitty asked me to have a discussion about the birth and marriage certificates with your man of business in London."

"I know. He called. What did he have to say?"

"It was just as you said, Your Lordship. When he took over your business matters, he performed an audit of your records here at Castle Rutledge. That's when he discovered their existence. After he brought them to your attention, you went in search of your brother. Found him in Robert."

"That's absolutely correct." He cast a fulminating glance toward Robert. "I hope that puts paid to all this nonsense as to whether Robert's my true heir."

"Unfortunately, Sir, there are questions," Ned said.

"What sort of questions?" Lord Rutledge demanded.

"The registry has no record of your father's marriage to Susan Rutland."

"It was never filed?" Robert asked, dismay clear in his voice.

"Apparently not," Ned said.

"Where does that leave us?" I asked.

"Well," Ned said. "I'm no expert, but it does seem to question whether Robert is the legitimate heir."

"The Chancery Court declared it to be so," Lord Rutledge exclaimed, his face becoming ruddy. "There's no question Robert is my heir."

"Yes, Sir," Ned responded. What else could he say?

"No one will question the validity of the marriage," Lord Rutledge asserted once more. "Not after the Chancery Court ruled on it."

"Unfortunately, it provides a motive for you to have murdered Freya Poole," Robert said.

I let out a hard sigh. Robert could be rather myopic when it came to his investigations.

"How dare you?" Lord Rutledge exclaimed. "Insulted in my own castle, by Jove."

Oh, dear. His face had grown red. I had to lower the temperature in the room before he suffered an apoplexy. "Robert didn't say you'd done such a thing, Lord Rutledge. He's only saying Constable Merryweather could determine that is a motive. Isn't that so, Robert?" I pinned a hard gaze on my fiancé.

"Yes, that's what I meant, Sir. I did not intend to accuse you of the crime." But clearly, he had doubts.

"We'll just have to prove the wedding ceremony took place in another way," I said.

Hollingsworth cleared his throat. "That's where I come in."

"Please explain," I said.

"When Ned discovered the lack of documentation, he asked for my help which I am more than glad to give."

"Thank you, Hollingsworth. You're always there when we need you." When Robert was suspected of murdering his previous fiancée, I depended heavily on Hollingsworth to conduct the investigation. Its successful conclusion was due in large part to him.

"I live to serve." He paused for a moment before offering a further explanation. "After discussing what needed to be done, Ned and I settled on a plan of action."

That didn't surprise me. During the Great War, Ned had been commandeered by the War Department. We never knew what he did. The Official Secrets Act precluded his sharing any information. But with his intellect, the rest of the family guessed it had to do with strategic planning. He would have applied those same skills to the current circumstances and devised a plan. And Hollingsworth, a man who relished adventure, would have gladly volunteered for whatever that involved.

"Someone needs to be dispatched to the town where the marriage took place and locate a witness," Hollingsworth continued to explain. "There had to be at least one. As busy as you and Robert must be questioning suspects and such, you have no time to involve yourselves in that search."

"And, I can't stress this enough," Ned interjected, "Mother is seriously worried you won't make your wedding. The sooner you solve this murder, the sooner you can return to London."

"But that's—"

"Eight days away, Kitty. You have eight days to find the murderer."

Mother had a point. We needed to return to London as soon as possible. Unfortunately, so few days to find a murderer when we hadn't known the victim nor any suspects before our arrival at Castle Rutledge would challenge our abilities. But we couldn't leave. We had to solve the murder before we left. Constable Merryweather didn't have the experience that Robert had. He might very well simply go along with the evidence that presented itself and name Lord Rutledge as the murderer.

"Thirty-five years have passed, Hollingsworth," Robert asked. "How do you intend to find a witness?"

"Charm, perseverance. And the judicious use of my comeliness, of course."

Lord Rutledge laughed at the outrageous statement.

"Don't forget your modesty," I said.

He quirked a smile. "No one has ever accused me of that. But given my other assets, I should be able to obtain information from some of the villagers, especially those on the distaff side."

He had a point, once he turned on the charm, never mind blind them with his male beauty, few women failed to respond to him.

"There," Lord Rutledge exclaimed, his usual color restored. "Somebody who's on my side."

"I'm on your side, Sir," Robert asserted.

Before Lord Rutledge and Robert's war of words could escalate, the butler strolled into the room. "Dinner is served in the dining room."

"How wonderful," I exclaimed. I would have to thank Benton for his perfect timing.

By silent agreement, we did not discuss the investigation during the meal. With the butler and footmen present, it would not be a proper thing to do. After we enjoyed our coffee and cordials, everyone sought their rest. However, I did not allow Robert to go into his room alone. We needed to hold a discussion before things got out of hand.

CHAPTER 16

A TÊTE-À-TÊTE

*T*hankfully, Hudson was not in Robert's bedchamber. So, we did not have to go through the awkwardness of dismissing him.

"You're in my room," Robert said, sounding rather cross.

"Yes, I know." Ignoring his mood, I proceeded to explore the space. "It's quite impressive with its dark massive furniture as befits the heir to the title. And you have a sitting room as well. No mirrors, though." I approached Robert. "How do you dress yourself in the morning?" I had a full length one in mine.

"I manage. What do you wish to discuss, Catherine?"

Seemingly my attempt at lightness had failed. "Your attitude toward Lord Rutledge. He's your brother. Your very dear brother. Just because you're investigating a murder doesn't mean you get to treat him like a suspect."

He raked a hand over his hair. "He is a suspect. The only one as far as I can see."

"Freya Poole spread her poison through the village. Surely there are bound to be others, including her own brother."

"Nothing points in his direction," he snapped out.

"Because we haven't investigated his whereabouts! Once we do, we can rule him out or include him. In the meantime, you're in danger of alienating your brother."

He arched a disdainful brow. "Are you suggesting I treat him differently than any other suspect?"

Heavens! He was in a mood. But I was not backing down. "I suggest you treat him as innocent as he's entitled to under the law."

"Have I been that harsh with him?" An honest question, softer in tone.

"Yes, you have, Robert. I suspect it's because you don't want to appear prejudiced in his favor. But it's hurting him. It's hurting your fraternal relationship."

Robert did not immediately answer. Instead, he approached a sideboard in the sitting room which held several bottles. "Would you like something to drink? Whiskey, gin?"

"Whiskey, please."

He splashed generous amounts into two glasses and handed one to me. Once he'd taken a sip, he asked, "What do you suggest I do?"

"When Constable Merryweather interviews him tomorrow, don't interject yourself. Don't interrupt. Don't ask any questions. Allow the officer to conduct the interrogation."

Gazing into his glass, he said, "I can do that."

"A solicitor should be present as well."

"My brother has already arranged it. He's arriving in the morning train."

"Thank heaven!" I dropped into one of the chairs. "He

couldn't have murdered Freya Poole, Robert. You've seen him. He's weak as a kitten."

Robert worked his jaw. "He could have paid someone else to do it."

"Why would he do that?"

"He knows I'm his father's son. The resemblance is too strong. But am I the legitimate heir? With his resources, he could have falsified that marriage certificate."

"But why would he do that? He didn't even know you."

"Actually," he said, "that's not quite true."

"What do you mean?"

"He knew of me. He admitted it as such." Before I could ask how he'd learned that, he continued, "He showed me an article from a London newspaper. I'd done something he thought heroic."

"What was it?"

"I rescued a mother and child from a burning house. My photograph was in the paper. Even though my face was covered in soot, he noticed the familial resemblance. I think that's when the thought took hold of him."

"But he didn't know your antecedents. For all he knew, you were born of your adoptive parents."

"He could have done a spot of investigation at that time. Once he discovered the times fit, he could have hired a detective to look into my history. He had the birth certificate. That at least is real. So he already knew my mother's name. As we learned from the vicar's housekeeper, the whole village knew she was having an affair with my father. It wasn't a secret. But to legitimize me, he needed a marriage certificate. So he paid someone to create the false document, and then he buried it among those his new man of business found."

"Good heavens, Robert, what a fanciful imagination you

have. You do realize most of what you've just said is conjecture."

"It could have happened."

"Could have doesn't make it so."

He poured another generous splash of whiskey into his glass. "More?" he asked.

"No, thank you." My head was already spinning from the potent liquor and the wine we'd enjoyed at dinner. "What makes you think Lord Rutledge would have done this?"

"He needed an heir to inherit the title and the estate."

"He could have married at any time and gotten himself one the usual way."

"No guarantees a marriage would have resulted in an heir. And a wife would have put a stop to the bachelor existence he relishes."

My heart sank. Was this Robert's way of telling me he felt the same? That I would interfere with his bachelor ways? Suddenly, doubt assailed me. He was thirty-five, nearly thirty-six. Had he settled into an existence he enjoyed and now rued his marriage proposal? My eyes welled up with tears. "Is this your way of telling me you no longer wish to marry?"

He swirled around to face me so fast the whiskey splashed over his glass. "What?"

I came to my feet and faced him straight on. "If you're having second thoughts about me, about our marriage, now is the time to say so."

He slammed down the glass, took two steps, and embraced me. "How could you ever think that?"

I sniffed into his shirt. "It's not hard, Robert. You've been rather difficult the last few days."

He curled a finger under my chin and raised it. "I love you. I will always love you. You light the shadows of my dark soul. I will love you until my dying day."

"Oh, please don't talk about death," I said in a watery whisper. "We have enough of that at the moment."

He kissed my brow, my chin, my cheek before his mouth took mine in a heated kiss that took my breath away. For some time, he gave way to passion, and I responded in kind. Wrapping my arms around his waist, I tugged at his shirt so I could slip my hand beneath it to feel the warm flesh beneath.

For a short while, he allowed my hand to explore his firm stomach and strong back before bringing our kiss to an end. "We need to stop, darling."

"Our wedding is eight days away, Robert. Surely, we're allowed something."

"If we continue what we've started, the something will become everything. And that, my beautiful Catherine"—he kissed my nose— "we're saving for our wedding night."

"Oh," I whirled away in frustration. "This entire situation is ludicrous."

"I agree."

I turned back. "I beg your pardon!"

"Not you. Not us. The enquiry."

"Oh!" I'd misunderstood him yet again. "I'm sorry."

"Nothing to apologize for. This investigation has us both on edge."

With that I had to agree.

I smiled as he tucked the shirt back into his trousers. I'd rather mussed him up. "Hudson would be outraged to find you less than flawlessly attired."

Straightening his tie, he said, "What he won't see won't bother him."

"I don't think you should send him back to London."

He frowned. "Why not? I don't need a valet at Castle Rutledge."

"I think he can help with the investigation."

"How?"

"While you and I are busy questioning individuals in Chipping Bliss, he can conduct enquiries with the castle staff, especially the women. You know how much the maids in your London residence like him. More than likely, the castle ones will as well." Due to his flawless fashion sense, Robert's staff was the best dressed one around Hanover Square, something the female staff particularly appreciated. Once upon a time, Hudson had worked as the costumer for a theatre company. He'd first met Robert when he'd been suspected of murder. After Robert found the true culprit, he hired Hudson as his valet.

"What makes you think Hudson would go along with your suggestion?"

Fighting back a grin, I said, "Because."

He narrowed his gaze before reaching the obvious conclusion. "You asked him to come."

"I sent him a telegram."

"How? When?"

"After we received Ned's. I had the chauffeur take the message to the village post office." Where the telegraph office was located.

"And you didn't tell me?"

"I'm telling you now."

"After the fact."

"Better to beg for forgiveness than ask for permission." I wrapped my arms around my once more nattily attired fiancé. "You will forgive me, Robert? I really do think he will be a great asset."

He gazed down at me. "Of course I will, minx." After a quick kiss, he said, "Now, go off to bed. We have a long day ahead of us tomorrow."

"You will talk to Hudson and give him permission to stay."

"Yes."

"Goodnight, Robert."

"Goodnight, Catherine."

I slipped out the door, which apparently we had left ajar. Not that it mattered. No one would be around this late at night. Unfortunately, I was wrong.

"Good evening." Hollingsworth stood outside, leaning against the balustrade, blowing smoke from a lit cigar.

"What are you doing out here?"

"I wanted to discuss something with Robert."

"And you didn't make yourself known?"

"I knocked. Heard you talking. Decided to wait."

"Well, he's free now. Have at him."

"Goodnight . . . Catherine."

Just how much had he heard? Holding my head up high, I said "Goodnight, Hollingsworth." And then I walked away, no doubt with my cheeks all aflame.

CHAPTER 17

THE DRESSMAKER AND THE PUB

*T*he following day after breakfast, I said goodbye to Ned. As busy as Worthington & Son was, he couldn't be spared for more than two days.

After driving him to the rail station, the chauffeur returned to Rutledge Castle to drive Robert and me into Chipping Bliss. And then he proceeded with Hollingsworth to Upton, the village where the marriage between Robert's father and Susan Rutland had taken place. Finally, he would head to the railway station to meet the solicitor's train.

I did not join Robert at the apothecary. My female intuition would not be needed for that interview. Instead, I headed to the dressmaker shop. Past experience with my modiste had shown me this would be the best place to discover the town gossip about the murder victim as well as other tidbits of interest.

The proprietor was a lovely woman with flaming red hair who went by the name of Mrs. Bretton. As soon as I walked into the shop, she and her assistant Jenny welcomed me with open arms.

"Would you like some tea, dearie?" Mrs. Bretton asked. "We have some lovely biscuits as well. Mabel's Cozy Tearoom prepares them fresh daily."

"What a charming name. Yes, I'd love some." Even though I'd recently eaten breakfast, I gladly accepted the offer. Tittle-tattle was best lubricated with a cup of tea.

When I turned the subject to Freya Poole, Mrs. Bretton didn't hesitate to offer her opinion. "She was a regular curtain twitcher, she was, always into other people's business."

"Anyone in particular?" I asked after nibbling on a lovely biscuit.

"Well, as of lately, she had developed a romantic fixation on the vicar."

"Vicar Mayfield?"

"The very one. When he gently turned her down, she turned her vile ways on him."

"What did she say?"

"She claimed he and the curate enjoyed an unnatural liaison. At the vicarage, no less. Can you imagine? Vicar Mayfield is fifty if he's a day, and Mister Lawson is in his mid-thirties."

"How very shocking! How did the vicar respond?"

"He preached about false rumors every other Sunday. *A false witness shall not be unpunished, and he that speaketh lies shall perish*. That's from Proverbs 19. Not that it did a bit of good. Freya continued to spew her poison every chance she got."

"How perfectly awful." I sipped the delicious tea. "What about her brother? What's your opinion of him?"

"A wrong 'un, through and through. His father beat him

because he was slow. And Freya? Not an ounce of sisterly affection for him. She enjoyed watching the punishment."

Heavens! The woman had been downright evil. "Any inkling why she was that way?"

"Well, her mother abandoned them, left them to the care of that awful man. Rumor has it he beat her. I think Freya snitched on her brother to keep him from using the strap on her as well."

"Was anyone ever interested in her? In a romantic fashion?"

"Not really. Everyone knew her for a shrew. She was sweet on a man once, though. The former marquis. The very spitting image of your man he was, or so I heard. I was barely out of me leading strings at the time." That rather explained why she'd maligned Susan Rutland's character. She'd wanted the marquis for herself.

Once we exhausted the gossip, the dressmaker got down to business. "A fine lady like you must have a modiste in London. But is there something you'd like from the shop?"

"Yes, there is."

When I told her what I needed, her eyes grew wide. But soon, the saleswoman in her took over. "That can be arranged, dearie."

After spending an hour at the dress shop, I headed toward the apothecary to meet up with Robert. Along the way, though, I had to pass the pub. On a whim, I entered it, but not before asking a young boy who was sweeping the entrance to take a message to the apothecary and tell Lord Robert where I was. I gave him a shilling for his troubles, and he took off like a shot.

The publican took pride in his place as the establishment was quite clean. I took a table next to a window so I could spot Robert as he walked up. Within a minute of me taking the seat, a woman with long dark hair pulled back with a bow approached to take my order. "What can I do ye for, dearie?" Dearie seemed to be part and parcel of the local lexicon.

Smiling, I asked, "What do you recommend?"

"Are you hungry?"

"Well, I just had tea and lemon biscuits."

"You'll need something savory then. We have a right smashing chicken pie. Wash it down with some ale?"

"Sounds like just the thing."

"Is your man joining you?" Seemed the entire village knew who I was and who I was engaged to.

"Yes, he's likely to."

"I'll tell Cook to prepare two then."

She brought the ale right away after giving the order to the cook. Once she walked away, a man I knew to be Freya Poole's brother slid into the seat across from me. Going from the smell and sight of him, he hadn't shaved or bathed in quite some time.

"Buy us an ale, love?"

Since I wanted information from him, it was the least I could do. But the man could use some food. "And a chicken pie?"

"Prefer a pasty, love."

"And so it shall be." I waved over the server.

She cast a suspicious glance at Freya Poole's brother. "Everything all right, dearie?"

"Yes. Mister Poole would like a dark ale and a pasty."

She raised a brow, but she brought the ale over. Mister Poole drained half the tankard in one gulp. And then he wiped his mouth with a less than pristine hand. "Thank 'ee kindly."

Somebody had taught him manners. "You're welcome."

"You know me name."

"You were pointed out to me."

"By the copper, I reckon."

"Yes. Tell me about your sister."

"Mean-spirited she was. Never had a good word to say about anybody. Got me into trouble with our da more than once. After he died, she kicked me out of the house."

"Is that when you started getting into trouble?"

"No. Got into trouble before that. I ran away to escape the strap. Nowhere to sleep. Stole things to keep body and soul together. Gaol was better than sleeping in the rough."

Well, that certainly explained why'd he'd been arrested so many times.

After the server brought over his pasty. I gave him time to enjoy his food before asking, "Who do you think killed your sister?"

"The vicar. The lord at the castle. The undertaker. Could be anyone."

The first two I expected but the third? "Why would Mister Diggum kill her?"

"She discovered some secret about him."

"Like what?"

"You think she'd tell me?" He croaked out.

I spotted Robert and Constable Merryweather approaching which meant I had to finish my interrogation.

"You didn't kill her, did you Mister Poole?"

"Nah. Gaol is one thing; the gallows another. Not eager to get my neck stretched."

The pub door swung open, and Robert and Constable Merryweather entered. As soon as they spotted me, they made their way to my side. While the officer frowned the entire way, Robert's expression only signaled curiosity. Once he reached me, he asked, "Enjoying an ale?"

"Quite so. I also ordered two chicken pies for when you arrived." I pointed to the man seated across from me. "This is Mister Poole. I bought him a tankard of ale and a pasty."

Having finished his meal and the rest of his drink, Mister Poole came to his feet. "Thank 'ee kindly, Miss."

But I wasn't quite ready to let him go. "Did your sister have other relatives?"

"Nah. It was just the two of us."

"You might want to look into who gets her cottage then. It could be you."

"Doubt it. She'd leave it to anybody *but* me."

"It's certainly worth investigating. You'd have a roof over your head. You wouldn't have to sleep rough anymore."

A glimmer of interest sparked in his eye "Who would I ask?"

"I can look into it for you," Constable Merryweather offered.

Poole turned a suspicious eye on the constable. "You never got me into anything but trouble."

"The constable is trying to help you," I said. "You should take him up on his offer."

Poole's attitude changed. "Thank you kindly, Sir. I appreciate it if you would."

The constable pressed Mister Poole's shoulder. "Come with me."

Resentment flared once more in Poole's eyes. "I ain't going to the constabulary."

"We're not going there. I'm taking you to city hall. That's where the land records are kept." Turning back to Robert, he said, "Meet you back here in an hour. We need to discuss what we arranged." Had to be his interview with Lord Rutledge.

"That should work," Robert said.

Mister Poole followed the constable out of the pub, but not before he thanked me again.

"Well, that was interesting," Robert said as he started to take the seat Mister Poole had just occupied. Thinking better of it, he switched it with another chair nearby. As soon as he sat down, the server approached once more.

"Lord Robert, what would you like to drink?"

"Dark ale."

"Now, I would think a lad from Castle Rutledge would favor the Castle Rutledge Reserve."

"A bit early for whiskey. I thank you all the same."

She brought back his dark ale and both chicken pies.

"Smells delicious."

"I'll tell Cook. She'll be plump chuffed."

Once she walked away, I teased, "The lasses in this village are most attracted to you. I don't know how you will tear yourself away."

He arched a brow. "You know very well you're the only woman for me. Now eat your pie before it gets cold." With that, he picked up his fork and dug in. But I spotted his amused grin.

CHAPTER 18

THE CASTLE HOUSEKEEPER

*B*y the time we finished our meal, Constable Merryweather had returned to The Angry Swan. We waited while he enjoyed a pasty and a dark ale before heading to Castle Rutledge in his vehicle. Once we arrived, Mister Benton informed us Lord Rutledge and his solicitor were waiting for them in the study, so he and Robert proceeded there.

While the constable conducted his interview of Lord Rutledge, I sought out the housekeeper. As she was in her fifties, she had to have known about the former marquis. She was easily found as she was working in her office. The butler might have been closemouthed, as the best butlers often are, but I sensed the housekeeper was ready to talk. Thankfully, she did.

"I was a housemaid back in those days, Miss Worthington. Barely sixteen I was, but my da worked at the brewery and got me a position here at the castle."

"Were you pleased about it?"

She smiled and nodded. "Da did the best he could. But with five of us to feed, it was a struggle. Here, I had a roof over my head, lovely meals, and a bed of my own. So yes, I was pleased, Miss."

"How lovely. How did you rise through the ranks?"

"I have always been a hard worker. The former house-keeper noticed, and she promoted me to head housemaid. When she retired, she recommended me for her position."

"How long have you worked at Castle Rutledge?"

"Close to forty years, Miss."

"You knew the former marquis?"

"Oh, yes, a lovely man, he was. So kind to everyone. Lord Robert is so like him in many ways."

"Is he?"

"The resemblance, of course. It's quite striking. And he's kind to the staff. Very pleasant in the way he speaks. Just like the former marquis. We were that sad when he died."

"Did he live here all the time?"

She nodded. "He rarely traveled to London or anywhere else. He loved the Cotswolds. Many a rambling walk he would take in the evenings before supper."

"And now you have the current Lord Rutledge."

She immediately turned silent. It was one thing to go down memory lane, but another thing altogether to talk about the current holder of the title.

I would have to be careful how I approached the subject. "He's not here as much as his father?"

"No, Miss. He spends most of his time in London."

"So he leaves the running of the estate to his manager, I suppose."

"Mister Poston. Yes, Miss."

"How long has he worked for the estate?"

She glanced off into the distance. "Oh, must be twenty years or so."

So he'd been working here at the time the new business manager had discovered the birth and marriage certificates among the former marquis's papers. The estate manager would not have bothered with those as his job entailed the management of the Castle Rutledge estate.

"Does he manage the brewery as well?"

"Only the business side. A master brewer handles the whiskey production."

"I'd love to visit it someday."

"Ooh, best not, Miss. The heady scent will knock you on your—begging your pardon, Miss."

I laughed. "Nothing to forgive. I totally understand. Would you mind if I asked a personal question, Mrs. Collins?"

"As long as I may decline to answer it."

"Fair enough. Did you never marry?"

"No. Marriage would have taken me from the castle, and that I could never do." She gazed around the room. "I love Castle Rutledge. I could never leave it."

"You'll retire someday," I said softly.

"To a room I've chosen in one of the towers. I'll live there until my dying day."

A knock on the door paused our conversation. A house-maid as it turned out. She became quite flustered to find me in the room. "Begging your pardon, ma'am. I didn't mean to interrupt."

"Nothing to apologize for. We were just about done." I came to my feet. "Thank you for your time, Mrs. Collins."

Standing up as well, Mrs. Collins folded her hands in front of her. "If I can be of help in any way, Miss Worthington, please do not hesitate to ask."

"I will." And with that, I left the housekeeper's office and went in search of Robert. He was in the study by himself, making notes at the desk. The late afternoon sun streamed through a window lighting that perfect form of his. For a moment, I paused to take in his male beauty. Hollingsworth was just as handsome, but his pulchritude did not affect me the way Robert's did.

He must have sensed my entrance because he glanced up. "Catherine."

"Is the interview done?"

"Yes."

"How was it?"

"Illuminating."

"Where is Lord Rutledge?" I asked glancing around.

"He's resting in his chambers. The interview took a toll on him. He won't be joining us for supper either. He intends to eat the meal in his room."

"Oh, dear. Was it that awful?"

"No. But the questions delved into areas my brother preferred kept private. Unfortunately, that is the nature of interrogations. We're often asked questions we'd rather not answer."

When steps sounded behind me, I turned to find Hollingsworth. "How did it go? Did you discover something of import?" I asked.

"It went well, and I did."

"Let's discuss it in your chambers, Robert." After we collected Hudson, the four of us proceeded there not only to learn what Hollingsworth had to say but Robert and Hudson as well.

As Hollingsworth's news was the most important, I asked him to report first. He verified that the church and all its records had indeed burned down. Within two years, the church had been rebuilt. The vicar who would have married Robert's mother and father passed away several years after the wedding took place. A curate had also worked at the church. But he and the new vicar had not gotten along, so he ended up leaving Upton a few months after the former vicar died.

"What was the curate's name?"

"Leonard Thompson."

I jotted that information in the journal I'd been keeping about the investigation. "Did you find out where he went?"

"To a church in London. St. Mary The Virgin in an area known as 'Old Hayes'. It's part of Bromley."

I made a note of it. "I'll telephone Lady Emma in the morning and ask her to look into it."

"Some people in the village remembered him," Hollingsworth said. "From what they said, I gathered he would be over seventy by now. Probably pensioned off."

"Or dead," Robert said.

"Don't be such a pessimist," I said before turning back to Hollingsworth. "Let's hope he's still alive and his memory's intact. Anything else?"

"The fire was looked upon as suspicious. But nothing was ever proved."

"How very odd. Why would anyone burn down a church?"

"Even more important, why wasn't that marriage certificate filed?" Hollingsworth asked.

"Because it never existed," Robert said.

He was in a mood. "Nonsense. Of course it did. Is that all?"

"That's as much as I could find out. I intend to travel to the county registry office. Births, marriages, and deaths are recorded there. With any luck, we'll find proof of the marriage."

"Marvelous idea, Hollingsworth. Thank you for volunteering for that task. We'll table the discussion about the curate's whereabouts until we hear back from Lady Emma." I glanced down at my list. "Hudson, did you find out anything from the castle staff?"

"Being a toff's gentleman's gentleman, I'm regarded with suspicion and distrust. But I did make some inroads with one of the downstairs maids who suffers from an overabundance of freckles."

Hollingsworth kicked his feet forward and crossed his ankles. "Vanity thy name is woman."

"I beg your pardon," I said.

Hudson scrutinized Hollingsworth. "Is that a hint of hair loss I see, Your Lordship?"

"What?" Hollingsworth jumped up and glanced at his reflection in the full-length mirror that now stood in the room. "Where? I don't see anything."

"Sit down, Hollingsworth," I said, laughing, "Hudson's teasing you."

After he'd retaken his seat, Robert said, "Vanity, thy name is Hollingsworth."

"You should talk. You're the one with a fancy mirror in the room."

"Which I didn't have until today."

"I asked it to be brought to Lord Robert's chamber," Hudson said. "I can't dress him properly without it."

Hollingsworth resumed his earlier pose. "If you say so."

"Please continue your report, Mister Hudson."

"Thank you, Miss Worthington. I provided the house-maid with a recipe to lighten her freckles, a mixture of lemon juice and honey. Once I did that, she turned sweet as a lamb."

"What did she have to say?"

"The staff is very protective of Lord Rutledge."

"As well they should be," Robert said.

"The staff has quite a different opinion of his attendant, Nigel Saybrook."

"Nigel has been with him for years, accompanies him everywhere he goes," Robert said. "What do they object to with him?"

"He started out as a boot boy. His father was a day laborer who worked on the farm."

"Humble roots, but that wouldn't make him less of a man or someone worthy of respect," I said.

"You're right, Miss Worthington. But apparently, Nigel undermined another staff member to obtain a better position."

"Please explain."

"Years ago, a silver epergne went missing. After an extensive search, it was found in a footman's room. He claimed he was innocent. But given the evidence, Mister Benton promptly sacked him. Nigel was given the post."

"Criminals always claim they did not commit a crime, even when they're caught with the goods," Robert said. "So that's not unusual."

"Just so, Lord Robert," Hudson replied. "But there's more. Nigel then made friends with Lord Rutledge's valet who taught him the duties of a gentleman's gentleman. Months later, the valet fell down the stairs, breaking his leg. He recommended Nigel as a temporary replacement. He never returned to that position as Lord Rutledge thought Nigel was a better fit. After the former valet's leg healed, he was offered Nigel's footman position. But as he deemed it a demotion, he refused it and left. I sensed there was more to the story. But at that point, we were interrupted by Mrs. Collins who needed the maid for some task."

"Thank you, Hudson," I said. "That was very illuminating." Turning to Robert, I asked, "What about you, Robert? Is there anything you can add about Nigel?"

"My brother is pleased with his performance. As you've seen for yourself, Nigel takes very good care of him."

"Do you think he would have killed Freya Poole?"

"He's fit enough to help Lord Rutledge with his necessities. It would have taken little effort to carry Freya Poole to the church. But why would he kill her?"

"Because Lord Rutledge asked him to," I said. "That's the argument Constable Merryweather would use. Did that come up in his interview of your brother?"

"In a roundabout way, but nothing directly. The constable asked if he'd needed Nigel's assistance the night of the murder. My brother explained that after taking a sleeping powder, he slept the entire night."

"We'll need to find out if Nigel was in his room that night," I said. "The staff sleeps two to a room so the other servant might have noticed if he stepped out."

"Unfortunately, that won't work, Miss Worthington," Hudson said. "He has private quarters next to Lord Rutledge's as the marquis might indeed need his assistance in late hours."

"Bother," I said. "Nigel could have left the castle without anybody knowing."

"More than likely."

"But how would he have gotten to the village?" Hollingsworth asked. "A two-mile walk during the day is easily accomplished. But at nighttime, it's another thing altogether, especially if it was cloudy."

"There was a full moon that night, and he would know that road like the back of his hand. He could have done it."

"Indeed," Robert said.

A knock on the door stopped anyone from saying more. Turned out it was Benton announcing supper. The discussion would resume the next day after breakfast. But as it turned out, another matter took precedence.

CHAPTER 19

THE CURATE

Mister Lawson has returned. The missive penned by Constable Merryweather reached us while we were breaking our fast. *I've arranged an interview at ten today.*

We'd risen early that morning as we always did. Habits die hard even when we were far away from London. Given we had an hour before we had to leave, we decided to discuss the questions we should ask of the curate. As soon as we finished breakfast, we headed toward Robert's chambers, specifically his sitting room.

As soon as Robert closed the door, I said, "I can only imagine what the castle staff must be thinking with us retiring to your bedchamber after breakfast."

"The obvious I suppose," he said with a crooked smile. "You don't mind, do you?"

"That they think we're canoodling? Not at all. If anything, it enhances our reputation with them, don't you think?"

His brow wrinkled. "What do you mean?"

"Well, with your brother being unmarried the threat of the staff being turned out when he's no longer with us must loom large with them. But then here we are. Not only in love but rushing off to your room. They can only imagine one reason for doing so. More than likely, they take comfort that the Rutledge line will continue, and their livelihoods will be assured."

"I never even thought of that."

"Well, they certainly would."

"Maybe that is why we were welcomed so warmly when we arrived."

"That was probably a large part of the reason. The other would be that we validated their occupations. They spend their time going through the motions of cleaning and such. But since Lord Rutledge does not visit often, no one acknowledges their hard work. And it is hard, Robert. The castle is huge. The daily upkeep is tremendous."

"Are you suggesting we visit more often than my brother has?"

"Between your Scotland Yard duties and my detective agency responsibilities, it will be difficult, I know. But we'll need to find the time to visit at least once a quarter. The Cotswolds must be beautiful in the spring and summer."

"Not winter?"

"It would be terribly cold with not much to do."

"Except for the canoodling," he quipped.

"Inspector Crawford, is that a suggestion? Because if it is . . ."

"How about we get on with the list of questions we wish to address?" He asked taking a seat in one of the sitting room chairs.

With a sigh, I did the same. I would have engaged in our banter forever, but we did have a task to perform. It didn't take long to compile the list. But before we left, I telephoned Lady Emma at the detective agency and provided her with the details about the former Upton curate, Leonard Thompson. She promised to make this her highest priority and to telephone as soon as she had news.

Having taken care of that matter, we were soon on our way to the vicarage.

As before, we were warmly welcomed by Mrs. Reilly and Vicar Mayfield. We walked into the parlor to find Constable Merryweather as well as two other gentlemen there. They stood as soon as we entered.

"Mister Andrew Lawson, my curate," Vicar Mayfield said.

Good heavens! The curate resembled Adonis. Tall, blond, with eyes so blue they could probably see forever. He appeared to be about Robert's age.

"And I'm Bartholomew Sloane."

"The apothecary." Robert explained.

He'd met him, but I hadn't. "How do you do?"

"Fine. Thank you. I know you have some questions to ask of Andrew, so I'll take my leave." Turning to the curate, he said, "We'll talk again."

"Yes," the curate said.

"Til then." The apothecary tossed him a look that transmitted humor and something more. A strong friendship? Or something else? Unfortunately, it was so fleeting I couldn't interpret its meaning.

While Mrs. Reilly escorted him out, the vicar excused himself to return to his study. He was preparing his homily for Sunday's service.

"Yes, of course," Constable Merryweather said.

Mrs. Reilly bustled in with a tea tray, cups, and saucers, and her delicious scones.

"How wonderful. Mrs. Reilly," I said. "I have to admit I was hoping to taste these again. They're quite delicious."

"Ta, dearie. Well, I'll leave you to it."

"You have some questions for me?" The curate said retaking his seat on the wingback chair.

"Yes," Robert said. The constable had agreed for Robert to take the lead on the questioning. "I understand you were called away two days before . . . my mother's funeral was to be held?" I didn't miss the hesitation in Robert's voice. He was still having a difficult time referring to Susan Rutland as his mother.

"I received a note from supposedly a neighbor of my mother saying she'd taken a turn. So, of course, I told the vicar and left the same day."

"What do you mean supposedly?" I asked.

"It was not true. Mother, thank heaven, is as hale and hearty as ever. She wasn't ill at all." There was a note of surprise in his voice.

"Who allegedly sent the letter?" Robert asked.

"One of her neighbors. The poor lady was flabbergasted when I asked her about it. She had done no such thing."

"You believed her?"

"Yes. She had no reason to lie. Given it would take the better part of a day to return to Chipping Bliss and too late to assist with the funeral, I decided to stay for a couple of days. Mother needed some things taken care of at the cottage." He flashed a luminous grin. "She was very happy to see me as you can imagine."

Recalling Mother's joy at Richard being home, I said, "Mothers are if they haven't seen their sons for a long time. Do you visit her often?"

"Once a quarter or so. Not as often as I wish. My duties here are quite extensive. Vicar Mayfield depends heavily on me."

"Yes, I can see that."

"I understand you were the curate when the vicar was

hired? Did you never wish to be the vicar yourself?" Robert asked.

"No. I'm fine as a curate."

"What are your duties?" I asked.

"Many are the same as the vicar's. I visit the sick, sit with the dying. But Vicar Mayfield counsels those who are seeking spiritual guidance and of course he offers the homily on Sundays. I attend to the mundane church matters. Manage the calendars—weddings, baptisms, and such. Arrange with volunteers in the community so the church runs smoothly. Supervise the church ladies' committee and the children's choir. And of course manage all the events surrounding the high holidays."

No wonder he couldn't visit his mother as often as he wished. With all the duties he had to perform, he barely had a moment to himself. "You're quite busy."

"Yes. But it's something I dearly enjoy." A sad expression rolled over his face. What could have brought that on?

"Can you think of anyone who could have sent that note?" Robert asked.

"No idea. We have pranksters at Chipping Bliss. Young men or children who like to play tricks. But to my knowledge none has written that sort of notes. That would take the sensibility of an adult."

I felt the same way. An adult had done this. One who wanted him out of the way for the funeral. Vicar Mayfield didn't bother himself with the church activities. He was more concerned with the spiritual side of things. So he'd depended on Mister Lawson to handle the funeral details. When the curate had to leave, the vicar was left to manage all of it.

Although everything had been arranged beforehand—the organist, the flowers, the undertaker—it had proven too much for him. So much so, he'd taken the sleeping powders. The result had been that he'd overslept.

So the murderer had to have planned both things. Getting Mister Lawson out of the way and arranging for a stronger dosage of the sleeping powders. It would be easy enough to get into the vicarage. Vicar Mayfield didn't believe in locked doors.

"We have another question," Robert said.

"About the bottle of Castle Rutledge Reserve whiskey?" Mister Lawson asked.

"You've heard."

"How could I not? I understand the poison was introduced into that bottle."

"Yes. Do you still have the one you won in that foot race in 1919?"

"Afraid not." The curate grinned. "It's been long gone. It didn't make it past Christmas that year."

"Understandably so," Robert said.

I knew we wouldn't get much more from him, so I excused myself. There was something I wanted to discuss with the housekeeper.

She was in the kitchen stirring something on the stove. "Mrs. Reilly?"

"Hello, dearie. Do you need more tea or scones?" As before, she welcomed me warmly.

"No. Thank you. I was wondering if I could ask you a question."

"Of course." She turned down the fire, wiped her hands on her apron, and turned to me.

"You mentioned Susan Rutland sewed her wedding gown, but she never got to wear it."

"That's right."

"I was wondering if perchance you kept it. That's what I would have done if she were my best friend."

Her face flushed pink. "Well, as a matter of fact, I did. There was no one else who would treasure it as I have."

I pressed her hand. "She would have loved for you to have kept it, I'm sure. Do you still have it?"

"Aye. Carefully stored in my wardrobe. I wash the gown and the veil every few years or so. Air them out good and proper before storing them again. Why do you ask?"

When I told her, her eyes grew misty. "I think Susan would have loved that."

CHAPTER 20

AN ALARMING DISCOVERY

The reinterment of Robert's mother was scheduled for the next day. With more than a little trepidation, we made our way to the church. Vicar Mayfield met us at the entrance, and then we slowly entered the nave. Unlike last time, when the church echoed with emptiness, we were surprised to discover the pews were filled with congregants, some of whom we'd already met.

The grieving countenance of the vicar's housekeeper, Mrs. Reilly, was particularly touching. It was her very good friend she was burying today. Constable Merryweather was in attendance and so was Doctor Brightwell and the apothecary, Mister Sloane. To my surprise Mister Poole was there. He had cleaned himself up as he was wearing a suit, had shaved and shorn his hair. I offered him a brief smile.

The requiem that flowed from the organ was everything that was appropriate and quite beautiful. Mister Houghton must have abstained from the bottle so he could play.

Once the service was done, a solemn procession drove away from the church. Lord Rutledge, Robert, Hollingsworth, and I with Nigel next to the chauffeur rode in the Rolls. The Vicar followed us with Mrs. Reilly next to him. I was glad someone who'd known Susan Rutland would be there for her reinterment. She deserved that and more.

Members of the Rutledge family were buried, not in a mausoleum, but in the Rutledge cemetery. Lord Rutledge's father had been laid to rest next to his first wife. And now Robert's mother would be buried to his left. Her tombstone read, *Susan Rutland Sinclair, Beloved Second Wife to the Marquis of Rutledge. In their death they were not divided* with her years of birth and death.

While the Vicar read from the good book, Mrs. Reilly stood softly crying. She was not the only one. I was as well.

Once the Marchioness Rutledge had been laid to her eternal rest, we returned to the castle for our luncheon. Both the vicar and Mrs. Reilly refused our invitation to share our meal. They had their duties to attend to. None of us were very hungry, but it was best if we ate. Food tended to put a little heart into you.

After the meal, Lord Rutledge retired to his chambers where he intended to spend the rest of the day. Hollingsworth expressed a wish to visit the brewery and off he went. Robert and I spent the early afternoon in the library. Days ago, I'd discovered a map of Paris, so we took the time to plan where we'd go during our honeymoon. The Louvre, the Champs d'Elysee. Versailles featured prominently.

"I never asked. Why were you on the Golden Arrow that first day we met?"

"I was visiting a friend in Paris."

"Oh." A *chere amie* more than likely. I did not like to think about it, but Robert had enjoyed liaisons with beautiful women before we met.

Seemingly reading my mind, he offered me a crooked grin. "Not that kind of friend. A French policeman. Michel Leclère. We'd worked a case together."

"And you traveled all the way to Paris just to see him?"

"And Marie."

"I knew there was a lady involved."

"Marie is his wife. And she's an amazing cook. I was craving her Cassoulet."

"Truly?"

"Truly. We'll visit them when we're in Paris so you can taste it for yourself."

A knock on the library door interrupted our conversation.

"Forgive me, Lord Robert, a gentleman has arrived. He's asking to see Lord Rutledge. When I informed him His Lordship was not available, he asked if he could talk to you."

"What's the name?"

"A Mister Grantford Sinclair."

"Sinclair?" I asked. Robert's surname.

"Yes, Miss Worthington."

"Very well," Robert said. "Show him in."

"Maybe he's a distant cousin wishing to pay his respects," I said.

"There are none. Our living family members include only Lord Rutledge and myself.

It took but a few minutes for Benton to return with the gentleman. Older than Robert by a few years, but of similar height and coloring. Maybe he was a relation, although not an acknowledged one.

Robert stepped forward to shake the gentleman's hand. "Mister Sinclair, how do you do? I'm Lord Robert." It was the first time he'd referred to himself with that courtesy title.

"Actually, that's not quite right." The gentleman's smirk was in full display.

"What do you mean?"

"As you're not legitimate, you can't be Lord Robert. I, however, am."

"What the devil are you talking about?"

Mister Sinclair retrieved an envelope from the inside of his jacket. "My credentials. As you will see, I am the grandson of William Sinclair, the younger brother of the former marquis. As my parents were married, and your birth parents were not, I am the legitimate heir to Castle Rutledge and the Lord Rutledge title."

CHAPTER 21

A CLAIM IS MADE

"*M*ay I sit?" Mister Sinclair asked. "Train travel can be quite exhausting."

Robert was busy scrutinizing the documents handed to him, so I responded, "Please do. Would you like some tea?"

"Thank you. Something heartier would be welcomed as well. Luncheon was hours ago."

By the time a maid arrived with tea and sandwiches, Robert had finished his examination. "They appear to be in order. But how would your claim take precedence over mine?"

"As I stated, my documents are real."

"So are mine."

"I hired a solicitor to research your credentials, Mister Crawford. The birth certificate was duly registered. But the marriage one was not."

"What prompted you to investigate?"

"After my father's death two months ago, I discovered my

grandfather's death certificate among his possessions. Someone had added a notation 'Brother to the Marquis of Rutledge.' You can imagine my surprise as I knew nothing about it. And then I recalled a story that had appeared in the press. The current holder of the title had discovered an heir, supposedly you. The notion seemed shady to me when you considered Rutledge was rumored to be ill. So I hired a solicitor to look into it. Lo and behold he discovered no marriage certificate had been recorded in the registrar's office. Without proof, your claim is invalid. Now, as I've said, I've had a long day. I'd like to get some rest. Any room will do."

The cheek of the man!

"You'll have to find one somewhere else, Mister Sinclair," Robert said. "You won't be staying at Castle Rutledge."

Sinclair jumped to his feet. "Why the devil not?"

"Until your claim is verified, you will not be welcomed here. Now, I can ask the chauffeur to drive you to Moreton on Marsh. There are several inns there where you can stay."

Robert rang for the butler. He must have been waiting for the summons, because he appeared within a very short time. "Sir."

"Can you inform the chauffeur his services are needed? Mister Sinclair needs to be driven to Moreton on Marsh."

"Of course, Your Lordship."

We suffered Sinclair's company in silence while he ate several sandwiches and drained the pot of tea. An interminable amount of time later, Benton returned. "The vehicle is awaiting Mister Sinclair by the front gate. I will escort him there in person." The butler must have taken the measure of the man and decided he didn't want him wandering around the castle.

"Thank you, Benton," Robert said.

Sinclair stood, a pugnacious expression on his face. "I'll be back, Crawford, and then I'll take what's mine."

Robert looked down his nose at the villain. "I doubt you'll succeed."

Sinclair stuffed two sandwiches into his pockets and stormed out.

I waited a moment before saying, "That was rather unexpected."

"To say the least."

"What are we going to do?" I wanted to let him know he wasn't alone in this.

"Investigate his claim, of course." He glanced at his watch. "We'll need to ask your brother to return to the registrar's office." He glanced at his Rolex wristwatch. "It's past five, though. Will he be at the office?"

"Oh, yes. He'll still be at Worthington & Son."

We proceeded to the study where the telephone was located to make the trunk call. Along the way, we ran into Hollingsworth who'd just returned from the brewery. Rather than explain things twice, Robert asked him to join us. It took a few minutes to be connected, but we were successful. And just as I thought, Ned was still in the office. When we explained the circumstances and what we needed from him, he promised to investigate it first thing in the morning. He would call us back tomorrow afternoon.

"Do you think the man's claim is valid?" Hollingsworth asked.

"We'll have to wait to find out."

"If only that marriage had been recorded," Hollingsworth said. "One must wonder why it wasn't. Has Lady Emma called with news?"

"No, which is odd. She should have done so even if she had nothing to report."

A knock on the door prefaced Benton. In his usual tone, he announced, "Lord Robert, another visitor has arrived. Lady—"

But before he could finish, the lady herself rushed in. "Hello!"

"Lady Emma!"

"In the flesh."

Quickly assessing the situation, Benton asked, "Shall I alert Mrs. Collins to prepare a room?"

"Yes, please, Benton, and if you could serve afternoon tea now. I believe we're all in need of sustenance."

"As you wish, Miss Worthington." He bowed out of the room, closing the door behind him.

After ditching her gloves, hat, and coat, Lady Emma rushed forward to hug me. "How are you holding up?"

"As well as can be expected. Hollingsworth has been a great help."

"I've hardly done anything," he said.

"That's not true. You've carried out a time consuming enquiry which has been of great help. Robert and I are immensely grateful." Turning back to Lady Emma, I asked, "Will you be staying with us long?"

"For a couple of days, if you'll have me."

"Of course we will. We welcome your company." I grinned. "Robert has Hollingsworth, and now I'll have you."

"Thank you, dear Kitty, Robert."

"How's the agency?"

"It's slow going at the moment; otherwise, I wouldn't have come. Lady Aurelia and Mister Clapham should be able to manage any enquiries that come its way. If not, they'll telephone."

"Splendid. Did you get a chance to look into Leonard Thompson?"

"I did." But before she could reveal what she'd found, a maid and a footman entered with the tea trays ladened with a variety of sandwiches, scones, pastries, and fairy cakes, as well as pots of coffee and tea and cups and saucers."

His eyes lighting up, Hollingsworth rubbed his hands together. "Good. I'm starving."

Once I'd poured tea and coffee and everyone filled their plates, I asked Lady Emma, "What did you find? He's not dead, is he?" The thing I most feared.

She laughed. "No. He's quite alive."

I issued a sigh of relief. "Thank heaven for that."

"And he's not at all in his dotage. He remembers quite clearly what happened. Your parents married in the Upton church, Robert. So you can put your mind at ease."

"But why wasn't the marriage recorded?" He asked. "Did he say?"

"He most certainly did. On his way to the county seat to do so, he was set upon by a thief who stripped Mister Thompson of everything, including the church parish register."

"What an odd thing to do!" I said. "What would he want with that book?"

"Mister Thompson never found out. But he was at the wedding, Robert. He assisted the vicar. You have your proof." She ended with a triumphant grin.

"I'm afraid more than that will be needed at this point," Robert said.

"What do you mean?" Lady Emma asked.

Robert explained about Mister Sinclair. "If his documents are valid, he'll press his case through the courts. I can tell you as an officer of the law that witness accounts are not worth as much as official documents."

"But he's a man of the cloth!"

"It doesn't matter. Persons can be bribed."

"Where was he accosted?" Hollingsworth asked.

"Just outside Upton," Lady Emma answered.

The village Hollingsworth had just visited.

"Nobody at Upton mentioned that happening."

"It was thirty-five years ago," Robert said. "People die. Others leave. Probably not that many people alive who knew about it."

"I'll have to return there and see if anybody remembers anything."

"From thirty-five years ago?" Robert asked. "I doubt it."

"He has to at least try, darling," I said.

Once Lady Emma's room was ready, I accompanied her to her chamber. "You're welcomed at Castle Rutledge, of course. But I do wonder why you're here when you could have simply called with your report." A thought suddenly assailed me. "It's not the agency, is it?"

"The agency is fine. It's Marlowe."

I should have known. But what could have gone wrong? During our holiday at Brighton, they'd come to terms with each other.

"What did he do now?"

"He misinterpreted something. As you know, last Thursday I visited a gambling hell. Disguised as a gentleman, of course." After the investigation of the stray stickpin matter, she'd become quite adept at masculine disguises. So much so that she now felt comfortable taking on cases which required that skill.

"Regarding the Henley matter." Valuable pieces of jewelry had been stolen from Lady Henley. At first, she'd suspected a maid. But after our investigation, we'd determined her nephew, an inveterate gambler, was the culprit. And he tended to favor one particular club.

She nodded. "We knew her nephew would be there that day. Mister Clapham obtained the secret word to gain entry. So that night I donned my costume and traveled there."

"You wanted to catch him in the act."

"Most stolen jewelry is fenced. But the Henley collection

is easily recognizable. So he exchanges the pieces for gambling funds at the hell."

"How does Marlowe come into this?"

"Just my luck he was there with a friend. As soon as I spotted him, I tried to blend in with a group of rather bosky gentlemen. But it didn't do any good. He saw me, saw right through my disguise."

"Of course he did." Marlowe would have become infinitely familiar with it when she'd adopted that guise to search for his lost tie pin at a gentleman's club.

"Furious did not begin to describe him as he stomped over to me. When his ire drew unwanted attention, I suggested we leave. He escorted me back to the agency and waited until I'd changed into my lady's garments. And then he took me home. I have not spoken to him since."

"With good reason. He shouldn't have said anything, much less acted the way he did. He ruined your enquiry."

She shook her head. "Only my part in it. Mister Clapham remained behind and obtained the evidence we needed. Yesterday, I notified Lady Henley. She won't involve the police as it would draw unwanted publicity. Instead, she plans to buy back the jewelry from the gambling hell. Her nephew won't escape punishment, however. She plans to banish him to a Scottish Highlands property she owns where he'll be forced to earn his living or starve. Either way, he'll never darken her footstep again."

"Serve him right."

"I will never forgive Marlowe."

I doubted that vow would last long. But for now, she needed comforting. "Absolutely."

"I love him, but I can't marry him. He'll never be easy with my chosen profession."

Curling my arm around her shoulder, I hugged her. "I'm

so sorry, Lady Emma." As Shakespeare once said, the course of true love never did run smooth.

CHAPTER 22

A SURPRISE GUEST

To our surprise, Lord Rutledge joined us in the drawing room before supper was announced. "I heard a new guest had arrived. A beautiful one," he said offering Lady Emma a courtly bow.

Lady Emma curtsied in response. "I hope it's not too much of an imposition, Your Lordship." After she'd indulged herself in a long bath and a lie in, she appeared much restored.

"On the contrary, my dear, I'm delighted you have joined us. We'd been rather in the doldrums, you see."

"Thank you, Lord Rutledge. That's very kind of you to say so."

Benton arrived, and in his usual dignified manner, announced supper was served.

"Shall we?" Lord Rutledge offered Lady Emma his arm. After leading the way into the formal dining room, he placed her next to him as we arranged ourselves around the table.

"So, how's London?" He asked once the soup course was served.

"As always," Lady Emma said. "A little on the cold side but that's to be expected given it's autumn."

"Teeming with people, I expect?"

"Yes, very much so."

"I miss the sound of automobiles as they travel down the streets, the cries of vendors, the smells, the sights. It's far too quiet here," Lord Rutledge said in a melancholy tone.

Well, that rather explained why he preferred London to Castle Rutledge.

But he soon shook off his mood. "And Worthington House?"

"You've heard about Richard's arrival?" Lady Emma asked.

"Dickie, yes. He loved to dig up Mildred's roses when he was a boy."

"And to track dirt through the house," I added. "Or so I heard as I hadn't been born yet. The staff was always cleaning up after him. Not that it stopped him from doing it again and again."

"Edward should have known his future was in archeology."

"Especially after he read Anthropology at Oxford," I said.

"I did as well as I wanted to go exploring," Hollingsworth said. "But the Great War put my travels on hold."

"It put an end to Dickie's studies as well," I said. "But, strangely enough, it was the start of his wanderings. He signed up for the army. But before he could report for training, a government agency drafted him into service. They sent him on several missions. We never knew where or what they entailed. But as he always had a facility of languages we figured they put that to good use. Mother worried about him constantly. But once the hostilities ended, he thankfully returned home with not a scratch on him."

"How did he wind up in Egypt?" Lady Emma asked.

"In one of his missions, he made a connection with an archeologist who offered Dickie a position on his team. He couldn't accept it fast enough, much to Mother's regret."

"What is his prognosis?" Lord Rutledge asked. "Malaria can be quite debilitating."

"He's progressing nicely according to his physician," Lady Emma said. "And he's been venturing downstairs for longer periods of time. His budding friendship with Lady Mellie has done him a world of good as well."

"Really?" Hollingsworth asked. As Lady Mellie's brother, he would have an interest. "I had no idea."

"A lot has happened since you last visited Worthington House," Lady Emma said.

"I didn't want to interject myself into the Worthington family. Between Richard's condition and the wedding preparations, they have enough on their plate."

"You may not be a blood relation, Hollingsworth," I said, "but Mother considers you, and Lady Mellie, family. So don't allow outdated notions of propriety to keep you away."

As we were being served the meat course, Beef Wellington, a footman entered and whispered something into Benton's ear. After a labored sigh, Benton announced, "Another visitor has arrived, Lord Rutledge."

Good heavens! Who could it be this time?

Echoing my thoughts, Lord Rutledge asked, "Who?"

"Lord Marlowe."

Should have known. Wherever Lady Emma went, Lord Marlowe followed.

"He's probably not had his supper. Show him in."

It took but a few minutes for Marlowe to make his

entrance. "I beg your pardon, Lord Rutledge, for arriving unannounced. I did not mean to interrupt your meal."

"Nonsense, my dear boy. Take a seat. We're currently enjoying the meat course. I hope that's satisfactory."

"Yes, thank you."

A footman rushed forward to set a dinner service in front of Hollingsworth. In no time at all, Marlowe had a gold charger, a dinner plate, cutlery, a goblet of water, and a glass of burgundy in front of him."

"You took the train, I imagine," Lord Rutledge said.

"Yes, it was rather dusty. I apologize for joining you in all my dirt."

Lord Rutledge dismissed that comment with a wave of his hand. "You can bathe after supper. So to what do we owe the pleasure of your company?"

"Well, Sir, I have news we thought best shared in person."

"We?" Lord Rutledge asked.

"Ned and I, Sir. A rather alarming article appeared in the newspapers. As soon as I read it, I telephoned him and offered to help in any way I could. He suggested I travel to Castle Rutledge to inform you."

Good heavens! What now? "What is the news?"

"Sir," Robert said. "Maybe we should dismiss the staff before we conduct that discussion?"

"If you think it best," Lord Rutledge said. "Benton, if you please."

Once the butler and footmen had cleared the room, Marlowe explained, "The article reported that Robert's claim to the title is not legitimate, but someone else's is."

Bother! Grantford Sinclair must have provided his documentation to the London papers. Since they thrived on scandals, they would have jumped at the chance to write such a story.

A peeved Lord Rutledge turned to his brother. "Do you know anything about this?"

"Yes, Sir."

"Who is this person who purports to be the legitimate heir?"

"Grantford Sinclair, your uncle's grandson."

"My uncle? William died during the Boer War."

"But he apparently married before he departed British soil. His wife gave birth to a son who in turn married and fathered Grantford Sinclair. I telephoned Ned and asked him to investigate the matter. He'll call tomorrow with his report."

"I see. And you didn't see fit to inform me?"

"It happened but a few hours ago. As I didn't want to disturb your rest, I decided to defer that discussion until morning."

"Very well. There's no help for it. We'll have to wait until Ned telephones. But tomorrow I want a full report on every-thing you've discovered about the murder and this interloper."

"Yes, Sir."

"Let's carry on with our meal. No sense in letting the news upset us. If you could ring for Benton, Robert. I believe I'm ready for dessert and coffee."

The rest of the meal was as convivial a one as I'd ever experienced. You would never have known the sword of Damocles hung over us ready to end Robert's claim to the title and charge Lord Rutledge with Freya Poole's murder.

CHAPTER 23

AN INVESTIGATIVE COMMITTEE MEETING

*A*fter supper, we gathered once more in Robert's sitting room since it was a space where we could be assured of privacy. We not only had to offer our reports but share where the investigation stood with Lady Emma and Lord Marlowe. As both had a myriad of questions, the process took an entire hour.

"To sum up," Lady Emma said, "You've interviewed the vicar and the curate and the housekeeper, the apothecary, and the physician. Talked to Freya Poole's brother and the dressmaker."

"Yes. We still need to talk to the undertaker. Mister Poole said Freya had discovered something about him."

"We will," Robert said. "I expect it will be another scurrilous tale with no basis to it."

"But you haven't identified a suspect?" Lady Emma asked.
"No."

"What about this Nigel? Lord Rutledge's attendant."

"Unfortunately, we'll have to rule him out," Hudson said.

"Why?" Not that I thought he'd murdered Freya Poole.

"He spent the night in the arms of one of the kitchen maids."

"Truly?" I asked.

"Afraid so, Miss Worthington. I suspected as much from glances they shared during mealtimes. When she headed to the herbarium to collect cooking spices, I followed her. She admitted she was enjoying a liaison with Nigel. The night of the murder, she was sharing his bed."

"You don't really suspect Lord Rutledge of murder?" Lord Marlowe asked of Robert.

"He does seem to have the strongest motive."

"Why?"

"Freya Poole was threatening to tell everyone I was not legitimate and therefore not the heir to the title. She said she had proof."

"As you've explained she was always scandal mongering. She thrived on it. Anyone could have murdered her. An errant husband or wife. Someone doing a spot of blackmailing. It could have been anyone."

"Chipping Bliss has a population of over 1,000. We can't investigate every person she gossiped about."

"Lady Emma and I are here," Marlowe volunteered. "We can help."

"We certainly can," Lady Emma said, "But I think we need to look at the murder from another perspective."

"Such as?" I asked.

"What if somebody was seeking revenge for a past transgression? Maybe something Freya Poole said caused irreparable harm or laid a reputation to waste. Or destroyed an innocent life."

I glanced at Robert. "That's a tack we haven't taken."

"No. We were more concerned with current rumors, and who lacked alibis for the time when the murder took place."

"How would we go about finding out?"

"We talk to women," Lady Emma said. "There should be several with long memories of what happened in the village in the last ten years or so."

"Mrs. Reilly would. She knew Susan Rutland. But why would someone seek revenge now as opposed to when the gossip was spread?"

"Maybe they didn't find out until recently, or someone held on to a secret until the present."

"Such as?"

"A dying person could have sworn to do so. But on the verge of facing their maker may have decided to clear their conscience."

"Yes, I can see that. I'll visit Mrs. Reilly in the morning. Lady Emma can chat up women in other places." After breakfast, of course. We wouldn't want to go forth with empty stomachs.

"Chat up women?" Marlowe asked. "And where would you do that?"

"Not to worry, Marlowe," Lady Emma said. "I know just the place."

"Fine," Marlowe answered. "What about me? What do you want me to do?"

"Go to Upton with Hollingsworth," I said. "You'll need to track down the witnesses to the marriage. Their names are on the certificate. They should be easy to find."

"It won't take both of us to perform that task," he said.

"No. But the other one will be. We need to find out whether anybody remembers the curate being assaulted."

"From thirty-five years ago?" Marlowe asked. "I don't see how anybody would."

"Upton is even smaller than Chipping Bliss," Hollingsworth said. "Most of its residents have been there their entire lives. I don't think it will be difficult. Someone is bound to remember."

"But what good would it do to find someone who recalls the incident?" Marlowe asked.

"Maybe they know who assaulted the curate. It could be a highwayman with a reputation."

"Like Dick Turpin, you mean? Does that sort of thing still happen?"

"Maybe not now. Automobiles put a stop to that. But thirty-five years ago, the curate would have traveled on horseflesh."

"Actually, it was a cart," Lady Emma said. "He was to bring back goods for the church. The thieves took everything, including the cart, the horse, and his clothes. And, of course, the church register. He was found by some travelers. After lending him some clothes, they delivered him to the Upton church. He didn't recall their names." Lady Emma yawned. "I beg your pardon. It's been a long day."

"You'd better seek your rest, Lady Emma. We'll see you in the morning."

"Yes, I think I'd rather."

"May I escort you to your room?" Marlowe offered.

"No, thank you. I can find my own way. Good night."

I sent a look to Robert who correctly interpreted the glance. "Hollingsworth, how about a game of billiards?"

"Capital!" And off they went while Mister Hudson bid goodnight as well.

The only ones who remained in Robert's chambers were Marlowe and I, just as I intended. "Marlowe?"

"Yes."

"You know what you did was wrong."

"You mean the bit about me interfering with Lady

Emma's foray into the gaming hell?" He wasn't slow to pick up on things.

"Yes, that bit."

"She was in a dangerous place. Something could have happened to her!"

"She was not alone. Mister Clapham was there. If someone tried to assault her, he would have stepped in. And she knows how to handle herself. She carries a knife and a handgun when the occasion calls for it."

"Does she know how to use them?"

"Yes, Mister Clapham trained all three of us lady detectives."

"But would she use them if she was in peril? There's a difference between practice and a real threat."

"You need to have that discussion with her, not me."

Leaning forward, he dropped his hands between his legs. Despondent did not begin to describe him. "Difficult, when she's avoiding me." Suddenly, he glanced up, a spark in his eyes. "Maybe I should accompany her tomorrow when she visits Chipping Bliss?"

I didn't say a word, merely gazed at him.

"Or maybe I shouldn't."

"You're learning, Marlowe. I'll give you that." I came to my feet. "I'm off to seek my rest. You might want to join Robert and Hollingsworth in the billiards room. They're probably expecting you."

"I'll do that. About Lady Emma." The man was relentless.

"I'll see what I can do. No promises, though." And then we proceeded on our separate ways.

Tomorrow was bound to be daunting. But I didn't expect what we eventually found.

CHAPTER 24

UPTON FINDINGS

*R*ight after breakfast the following morning, Hollingsworth and Marlowe left for Upton while Lady Emma took aim at Chipping Bliss. Robert and I remained behind as we wanted to strategize our next move. Good thing we did. Because as we were doing just that, Ned telephoned.

"Ned. How are you?"

"Busy as always. Mother, Father, and Dickie send their love. You can guess what Mother's additional message is."

"Hurry back?"

He laughed. "She gets it in one. The house is teeming with people coming and going, half of whom I don't know who they are. By the way, Mother decided to add swans."

"Swans?" Heavens! "Not real ones I hope."

Robert made a face, probably at the mention of the avian creatures.

"No. Ceramic. They'll function as the table centerpieces for the floral arrangements."

"That doesn't sound too outrageous."

"I'll explain later," I mouthed to Robert. "So what did you find out, Ned?"

"Well, the documents are real. They were properly registered."

"Oh." I couldn't help but feel disappointed.

"But I could not locate a marriage record for William Sinclair during the appropriate time period. I did find his death certificate and his military records. They listed his brother as next of kin. No mention of a wife anywhere."

"Well, well, well." I shared that information with Robert.

"If William Sinclair was not legally married, then Grantford Sinclair can't inherit the title or the estate," Ned said.

"You're certain of this, Ned?" Robert asked.

"As sure as I can be. I've turned the matter over to our solicitor. He'll have a clerk dig through the records. But he says it appears to be a false claim."

"Well, that's a load off our shoulders. If you hear different, please telephone."

"I will. And Kitty—"

"Yes, I know. Hurry back."

"Well, that's that," I said after putting the candlestick mouthpiece back on the holder.

"As far as his claim is concerned," Robert said. "I still have to validate mine."

"We should head to Upton."

"I thought you planned to talk to Mrs. Collins."

"I can visit the vicar's housekeeper anytime. Since it appears that Grantford Sinclair's claim is invalid, we must prove yours is legitimate. That means locating the witnesses to your parents' marriage, and with any luck, the parish register. Between the four of us, we should be able to do that."

"The murder investigation should take precedence, Catherine." That was the Chief Detective Inspector talking. But I had an answer to that.

"We'll do that as well. We need to verify the curate did not leave that village the night before the funeral, and that needs to be done at Upton."

"Fine." He was not entirely comfortable with my reasoning. But my gut told me the curate was the key to solving the murder. And it was rarely wrong. "We can enjoy a luncheon at their pub. Once we feel peckish, that is."

He laughed and drew me into his arms. "Do you ever stop thinking about food?"

"Yes, when I sleep."

After a round of very satisfactory snogging, we were on our way to Upton. An even smaller village than Chipping Bliss but built differently. The most important buildings— the church, the post office, the local pub—had been arranged around a square in the center of which a fountain flowed. It took no time to find Hollingsworth. He was in the rectory's parlor discussing the former curate's assault with the Upton Church vicar.

As soon as Hollingsworth saw us, he came to his feet. "Vicar Crumb, please allow me to introduce Lord Robert Sinclair and his fiancée, Catherine Worthington." He turned to us. "I've provided the vicar with the details regarding the investigation."

"So pleasant to meet you, Lord Robert, Miss Worthington," Vicar Crumb said. An older gentleman of around sixty going by his thinning grey hair. Neither short nor tall, he had a quite pleasant face and a ready smile. "Please join us. We're enjoying tea and biscuits."

"Thank you, that's lovely." Robert and I settled ourselves in the small sofa that faced the vicar.

After we'd availed ourselves of the refreshments, Hollingsworth caught us up on what the vicar had shared with him. "Vicar Crumb came to Upton as a curate. He replaced Mister Thompson."

The curate who'd been assaulted and robbed of his possessions including the church registry.

"Although he was not here during the time of the previous curate, he heard about it."

"Indeed, I did," the vicar said. "It's all the good people of Upton could talk about when I came to this parish."

"Did they ever catch the thief?" I asked.

"Years later. He robbed one too many and was caught. He ended up in gaol, of course. Died there as far as I know."

"What about his stolen goods?"

"None were ever found, I'm sorry to say. Apparently, he'd taken them to London to be fenced."

"We learned the church burned down around that time, but it was rebuilt after the fire?"

"Indeed, it was. We held services in the public house for two years. But the good people of Upton raised funds to build a new worship house. A humble building but we're rather proud of it."

"As you should be," I said.

"I gather you're trying to find proof of your parents' marriage, Lord Robert."

"Yes, it's rather important."

"Lord Hollingsworth explained."

"You will wish to visit Mrs. Helena Lawson then," the vicar suggested.

"Any relation to the Chipping Bliss curate?"

"His mother."

"Why do you suggest we visit her?"

"She worked at the church during the period you're interested in. She might have knowledge of your parents' marriage."

"We'll do that. Thank you. What do you know about Mister Lawson?"

"He was my curate for a few years, two or three as I recall, before circumstances forced him away from us. He was excellent at his position."

"Or so we've heard." I hesitated a moment before asking the next question. "What drove him away from Upton?"

"You've met him?"

"Yes, we have."

"A rather handsome lad, wouldn't you agree?" He said with a grin.

"Yes, he is." Both Robert and Hollingsworth shot me equally amazed looks.

"I'm not blind, Robert. I can appreciate a good-looking gentleman even if I'm in love with you."

The vicar chortled. "You're not alone, Miss Worthington. Half the Upton female population attended Sunday service to catch a glimpse of him. And he is as kind as he is handsome." His voice took on a serious tone. "I hated losing him."

"What happened?"

"A young lady fell in love with him. She wasn't of sound mind, the poor dear. She pursued Mister Lawson relentlessly. Wouldn't allow him to breathe. Unfortunately, she got herself in the family way. Seeing an opportunity, she named him as the father. He denied it vehemently, of course. When she gave birth to a child who looked nothing like him, she finally confessed the truth. Turned out the father was an itinerant worker who'd passed through town several months before. Faced with a reality that was not what she'd asserted, she went quite mad. Her mother had no choice but to put her in an asylum. But unfortunately, the damage had been done.

145

Tongues wagged, and he was labeled a seducer of innocent young women. Mister Lawson saw no choice but to leave Upton."

"How very sad."

As we'd gathered as much information as we could from the vicar, it was time to say our goodbyes. Coming to my feet, I said, "I imagine you're quite busy with church matters, so we'll take our leave."

Robert was not slow to echo my sentiments. "Thank you for your time, Vicar Crumb. We sincerely appreciate your assistance."

The vicar stood as well. "You're welcome, my children. My door is always open. If you need me, I'll be here or at the church."

Since by that time the three of us were more than a bit peckish, we headed to the public house after we left the rectory.

It being early afternoon, the public house had few patrons. We were warmly received by the proprietor and the server who turned out to be his wife.

"What do you recommend?" I asked. "We're all famished."

The server did not hesitate to respond. "Steak and ale pie with a dark ale to wet your whistle."

"Perfect!" I exclaimed. "Do you have something we can munch on while we wait for the pie?"

"Pretzels. Freshly baked this morning, mind you."

"That will do. Thank you."

The ale nicely brazed us and the pretzels were delicious. In no time at all, we wolved them down. Even as we were doing so, the server returned with the steak and ale pies. But they were piping hot. While we waited for them to cool down, we discussed in low voices what we'd just heard.

Once we finished that discussion, I said, "I can't help but think Mister Lawson is the key to this whole thing."

"What do you mean?" Robert asked.

"We know he was driven away from Chipping Bliss with a fake note."

"Yes."

"Now, Vicar Mayfield relied on him to handle the church details. He told us so. And the funeral was of particular importance to him. So it stands to reason Mister Lawson might have been in the church late in the evening before the funeral was to take place to assure everything had been done."

"So the murderer arranged for Mister Lawson to be away, so he could get on with killing Freya Poole."

"Yes. That was part of it. But what if there was an additional reason?" I asked.

"Such as?"

"To ensure Mister Lawson wasn't blamed for the crime."

"Explain," Robert said.

"He was driven out of Upton because of malicious gossip, that some of the Upton residents believed. And here was Freya Poole spreading vicious rumors about him in Chipping Bliss. He would have made a likely suspect of the murder. And more than a few of the villagers would believe he had something to do with it."

"Except for the fact he wasn't in Chipping Bliss the night of the murder," Hollingsworth added.

I banged the table. "Exactly."

The server reappeared like a shot. "More ale?"

"Uh."

"Yes, please," Robert said. "Another round." The server left to fulfill the order.

"We don't want to get bosky, Robert," I whispered. "We have an investigation to conduct."

Hollingsworth laughed. "Lass, it would take more than two tankards of ale to get me to that point. And may I

147

remind you of your fiancé's capacity for drink? At Oxford, the man drank me under the table on more than one occasion."

I gazed in amazement at Robert. "You didn't?"

"I did," he responded with a grin. "I had to get him in that state before he would allow me to take him back to his rooms. And he refused to drink alone."

The things one learned. After the server returned with three more tankards, I said, "Where was I?"

"The curate being away from Chipping Bliss so he could not be blamed for the murder," Robert said.

"That's right." I shouldn't have been surprised he'd summarized my words as well as he had. He was a Chief Detective Inspector at Scotland Yard, after all. He knew how to listen and how to phrase things.

"Who would have wanted to do that?" Robert asked.

"Someone in love with the curate who didn't want to see him hurt again."

"A woman couldn't have carried Freya Poole all the way to the church," Hollingsworth pointed out. "She wouldn't have had the strength."

"It could have been a woman. A strong one. I doubt Freya Poole was carried from her house to the church. More than likely she was put in a conveyance of some kind. Not an automobile. Someone would have noticed it even in the dark of night." Automobiles tended to be big, noisy things.

"A cart?" Hollingsworth suggested.

"Or something similar. Freya Poole's wrists were bruised. She could have been dragged outside her home, lifted into a cart, and taken to the church. Once there, the murderer would have reversed the process, propped her up in the sacristy, and dressed her in the church vestments."

"But that would point to the curate, wouldn't it?"

"Not if he wasn't there. He couldn't have been at Chipping Bliss and Upton at the same time."

"And that means we'll need to verify his alibi."

"Once you gentlemen finish with your ale, that is."

All I got in response were equally amused grins.

Men!

CHAPTER 25

MRS. LAWSON

*O*ne glance at Mrs. Lawson and we knew from whom the curate had inherited his stunning looks. Gorgeous blonde hair plaited on top of her head with the same piercing blue eyes he possessed.

We mentioned the vicar to introduce ourselves. He'd given us permission to use his name. After Mrs. Lawson showed us to her front room and invited us to sit, I said, "Thank you for talking to us."

She wasted no time bringing the conversation around. "This is about my Andrew, isn't it?"

"Yes, ma'am. It is."

That piercing gaze drilled into me. "I will hear no vicious rumors spoken about him. He's a good man and the best son a mother could have."

The poor woman. She probably had suffered through many a nasty comment about him. No wonder she felt so protective about her son. "So, we hear. Tell us about him."

"He was a hard worker around the farm. Even when he was little, he always helped out. My husband" —she swallowed hard— "died when Andrew was fifteen. He ended his studies at the village school to take over his father's duties. We would not have been able to keep body and soul together if he hadn't. And then one day the vicar came calling. He needed help at the church. He promised Andrew generous compensation, so he went to work for him. The vicar instructed Andrew in the ways of the church. When he turned twenty, he became a curate. Proudest moment of my life."

"But then he left?" I asked.

"Yes, Ellen Goodson started spreading lies about him. Claimed he was her baby's father. It wasn't true. My son would have never done such a thing. He's everything that's good and proper." She breathed out a hard sigh. "In the end it was proven not true. But the lies had taken root. People were pointing fingers at him. And so, my Andrew had to leave. That day was beyond sad." She wiped a tear from her cheek.

"But he's not that far away. He visits you," I offered by way of comfort.

"Yes, he came just last week. But that I imagine you already know."

"We do indeed."

"He arrived last Tuesday. Stayed for five days."

"He never left?"

"No. Too much to do around the cottage. I've let things go, you see. I'm not as young as I used to be. There are plenty of others who saw him. In case you don't believe me."

I had no doubt her neighbors would confirm what she said.

"If you don't mind me asking, Mrs. Lawson? How did he arrive?"

"Well, there's a bus between Chipping Bliss and here.

That's the way he usually comes. But last week, a friend drove him."

"What friend?"

"Mister Sloane, the apothecary. They're great friends."

I purposefully kept my gaze from wandering to Robert. But I knew he'd picked up on the name.

"It's good that he has such a great friend."

"Oh, my Andrew never lacked for them. All the boys wanted to be his mate. I can only hope he finds new ones in London."

"London?"

"He's applied for a new position there. The gossip in Chipping Bliss about him and the vicar is wearing him down. He figures he'll fare better in London."

"Will you go with him?"

"No. I've lived all my life in Upton. I'll die here as well."

"I'm so sorry."

"I just hope he'll find friends there who treasure his kindness." Her gaze wandered to Hollingsworth and Robert. "I imagine the two of you are best mates."

"You can tell?" Robert asked.

"Oh, yes. You've known each other a long while, haven't you?"

"Indeed, we have, Mrs. Lawson. We attended Oxford at the same time."

"I would have loved for Andrew to have gone to university. He's a wonderful scholar. Always has his nose in a book."

The maid who'd opened the door for us stepped into the room. "Would you like your tea now, Mrs. Lawson? I have to get on with my work."

"Yes, please, Lettie. Bring enough for my guests."

"Oh, none for us, thank you. We've just enjoyed a late luncheon."

Once the maid left, Mrs. Lawson said. "You'll have to

excuse Lettie. She's a little abrupt. Her husband used to beat her, the poor soul."

"How awful," I said. Just the thought of it made me ill.

"He paid his dues at the end, though. Died in jail. He considered himself a highwayman, robbed travelers on the road."

Robert, Hollingsworth, and I sat up. Had we stumbled upon the evidence we sought? "Did he by chance rob the curate, Mister Thompson?"

Lettie bustled in with the tea service.

"He was certainly suspected of it," Mrs. Lawson said. "But it couldn't be proven."

"Oh, he most certainly robbed Mister Thompson," Lettie said dropping the tray on the small table with a clatter.

"How do you know?" I asked her.

"I saw it with me own eyes. What he wanted with that poor curate's possessions is beyond me. He took his cart, his clothes, even his medallion."

"What medallion?" I asked.

"The one the church gave him. That's what Arnie took to London. He chopped up the cart for kindling to keep us warm. Sold the horse to someone. Can't remember who. And then he went off to London to sell the rest. He didn't sell the book, though."

The register. It had to be. "What book?"

"The parish book. He thought it would bring a penny or two in London. But I couldn't allow him to do that. It would be a sin, you see. So I hid it from him. He beat me when he couldn't find it. Beat me good and proper. But I never told him." She ended with a grin.

The poor woman. What she must have suffered at the hands of that brute. "Do you still have it?"

"Oh, aye. It's under me bed. I pray on it every night. Can't read it. Never learned how. But I know it has holy words in it."

As kindly as I could, I asked, "May we see it, Lettie?"

Unfortunately, she immediately became suspicious. "Wot fer?"

"Well, it has something very important in it."

"Wot?"

"Proof of my parents' marriage," Robert said. "It's very important, Lettie."

We hardly drew a breath while she pondered her decision.

But finally, she said, "Oi guess you can look at it. But you can't have it, mind you."

If indeed it was the parish book, we would cross that bridge at that point.

All of us, including Mrs. Lawson, followed her as she led the way to her bedroom. Her bedspread was almost threadbare, indeed most of her possessions had seen the ravages of time. But the room was pristine. There was hardly a speck of dust to be found.

She bent to fetch the book from underneath the bed. Robert started to help, but I warned him off by shaking my head.

She dragged it out and carefully placed it on her bed. "I keep it clean, you see."

Such an unassuming book, and yet it held the key to Robert's past. And his future. "I do, Lettie. You've done a wonderful job keeping it safe."

"Thank 'ee."

"May I look through it? I promise not to damage it."

She bobbed her head even as she wrung her hands.

I had the marriage date memorized. Robert's parents got married early January 18, 1888, the year Robert was born. Our wedding would be held on his birthday, the 26th of

October. I carefully turned the pages until it came to the right one. And there it was, the marriage of Susan Rutland, spinster, to Robert's father, Marcus Sinclair, bachelor. I gazed at Robert with tears in my eyes. "There it is, darling. Proof."

"I could have told you that, Miss Worthington," Mrs. Lawson said. "I witnessed their wedding."

"But the witness name on the marriage certificate is Helena Patterson."

"My maiden name. But I've gone by Nellie my entire life." She said smiling from ear to ear. "No one could deny you're your father's son, Lord Robert. You look exactly like him."

The negotiation to take the church book with us took another half an hour, and we had to get Vicar Crumb involved. He explained to Lettie that the book rightfully belonged to the church, and it'd be a sin, not to mention against the law, to keep it in her possession. He gave her another book, the King James Bible, which he blessed before handing it to her. When he told her it would keep her safe the rest of her life, she clutched it tightly to her. And smiled.

Just as we were leaving Mrs. Lawson's cottage, Marlowe appeared. "I've been looking all over for you."

"Glad you found us."

"I've drunk enough tea to sink a ship, but unfortunately discovered nothing new."

"We did. We'll explain along the way." We'd asked Lord Rutledge's chauffeur to meet us at the church at five and it was nearly that time now.

The vicar allowed us to take possession of the parish register. We would carry it with us to London so the marriage of Robert's parents, along with all other events in the register could be duly recorded in the registrar office. We didn't know what that process would entail. But the important thing was we had proof.

"Well, I'll be," Marlowe said once we'd explained it to him on the return trip to Castle Rutledge. "She kept it all those years."

"She claimed it kept her safe. Apparently, her husband was arrested shortly after he assaulted the curate. She took that as divine providence because she'd rescued the book."

"She'll never want for anything in the future," Robert said. "I intend to reward her for safeguarding the parish book for as long as she did."

CHAPTER 26

BACK AT CASTLE RUTLEDGE

*U*pon our return to Castle Rutledge, Robert asked Mister Benton. "Is Lord Rutledge in his chambers?"

"Indeed he is, Lord Robert. He asked if you could please visit him as soon as you returned."

Robert turned to me and pointed to the first floor where all the bedchambers were located. "I'll just . . ."

"Go. He'll be glad to hear the news." I watched as he took the stairs two at a time.

"Any chance a luncheon could be served, Mister Benton?" Marlowe asked. "Afraid I missed mine."

"Of course, Your Lordship. Will the drawing room do?"

"We enjoy our meals there when it's only a few of us," I explained.

"I'll join you, if you don't mind." Hollingsworth said.

"So that would be two luncheons to be served in the drawing room?" Benton asked.

"Yes. Thank you, Benton," I said.

Marlowe and Hollingsworth headed off in that direction. Since that was where the spirits were kept, I imagined they planned to enjoy a tot or two of Castle Rutledge Reserve before their meal was served.

Before the butler could proceed to the kitchen to alert Cook, I needed to know something. "Has Lady Emma returned from the village?"

"She has, Miss Worthington. She's in her bedchamber."

Bother! I really wanted to talk to her as I wanted to find out if she'd discovered anything of note.

"She asked if you could stop by upon your return."

"Splendid. Thank you, Benton!"

"You're most welcome, Miss Worthington. Would I be allowed a personal remark?"

"Yes, of course."

"The Castle Rutledge staff is very happy Lord Robert, you, and your friends are here."

"Why, thank you, Benton. Please thank them, especially Mrs. Collins. We've been made more than welcome. Lord Robert and I look forward to visiting as often as we're able. Oh, and we'll bring as many of our friends as we can."

"We look forward to such visits. I'll let the staff know." After offering a deep bow, he headed off.

I climbed the stairs and headed in the direction of Lady Emma's room. After a quick knock, she opened the door herself, draped in the Oriental style robe Mother had gifted her for her birthday.

"What have you done to yourself?" I asked. She'd under-gone a transformation since this morning. Her hair was shorter, her nails were manicured, and her skin positively glowed.

"I visited Griselda's House of Beauty."

"Griselda's?"

She wrinkled her nose. "The name needs some work, I agree. But her services are wonderful, and so reasonably priced. Hair, nails, skin. Got the complete beauty treatment." She flashed her nails in front of my face. "Siren Red. Matches the lipstick and my toes." She wiggled those as well. "And she has the most luscious facial creams. What do you think?"

"Gorgeous. Your skin positively gleams."

"I should hope so. I spent three hours at the salon. Of course, that was not the only reason I was there. I wanted to hear all the village gossip."

"And did you?"

"Absolutely." Without pausing for breath, she asked, "Should we ring for tea? I'm famished."

"I'll do that while you dress."

Barely fifteen minutes later, one of the maids delivered a tray ladened with not only the tea service but all sorts of pastries.

"Ooh, I adore fairy cakes," Lady Emma said, biting into one. "You don't want one?"

"Better not. I have my wedding gown to consider. Mother would be highly upset if it no longer fit."

"Thank heaven I don't have to worry about that."

"You're one of my bridesmaids!"

"But they'll be looking at you, not me," she said taking another nibble.

"So what did you discover?"

"Well, we knew what a wretched gossipmonger Freya Poole was. But we didn't know the extent of her poison."

Over the next half an hour she detailed the lives Freya Poole had ruined. A young lady she claimed was having an affair with a married man. The post office mistress she charged with embezzling funds. And the worst of all. A young widow she said had killed her husband. The gossip became so vicious she had to leave the village. "There were more, but those were the worst."

"No wonder no one liked her."

"Everyone loathed her, Kitty. And apparently, she was doing a spot of blackmailing as well."

"Makes sense. She had no known sources of revenue as far as we could see."

"No one did a thing about it. It was all grumble, grumble, grumble until she went after the vicar and the curate. They're both much loved in the village. No one believed a word of it, of course. I mean the vicar is over fifty years old and the curate must be no more than thirty."

"Actually, he's thirty-five. We met his mother."

"Did you really?"

"Yes. Go on."

"Well, the villagers got together and formally complained to the village council. The leader visited Freya Poole but came away with a flea in his ear. She told him she had a right to say what she had to say, especially since it was the truth. As you can imagine, that did not go over well. The villagers resumed their discussions to plan their next step, including a good old-fashioned witch burning. Would you believe it? But then she was murdered."

"And that solved the problem of Freya Poole."

"Indeed. I'm afraid the pool of suspects is rather a large group. I don't know how we'll get through them all." She sipped her tea. "Did you find anything of import at Upton?"

"Yes, we did. We located the parish register. We now have definite proof Robert's parents were married."

"That's wonderful!"

"The Upton vicar allowed Robert to borrow the book so all the marriages, births, and deaths during the period of time registered in it can be added to the registrar's records in London."

"But where did you find it?"

"Beneath a woman's bed." The entire story poured out of me.

Lady Emma felt the same sympathy for Lettie I did. "The poor woman. What a wretched life she's led."

"She won't ever suffer hardship again. Robert is settling a comfortable pension on her for safeguarding the register as well as she did."

"What a wonderful thing to do." She sipped from her tea. "Um, was Marlowe with you?"

"He was there asking questions. But we didn't meet up with him until we were ready to leave. He and Hollingsworth are enjoying a light meal in the drawing room if you care to join them."

"I don't think so."

"He's sorry for interfering with your investigation."

"Not sorry enough not to do it again."

"Actually, he knew you were in Chipping Bliss by yourself. As much as he wanted to barge in, he didn't."

She sighed. "Maybe there's hope for him."

"He worries for you. He doesn't want you to get hurt."

"And what could I possibly do about it?"

"Well, I suggest you discuss your process with him. Tell him you never venture on dangerous missions by yourself. You and I always take Mister Clapham with us whenever the occasion calls for it. And you might want to explain your training on weapons."

She arched a brow. "Why should I? My lady detective responsibilities have nothing to do with him."

"Because you love him, and he loves you. If you ever marry, he will need to know you're taking appropriate precautions."

"Do you discuss your process with Robert?"

"I have. I also discuss my investigations with him when I have need of his expertise."

"But you didn't tell him about that last foray during the jazz club murder investigation."

"I did not, but I did take Mister Clapham with me."

"And yet, you ended up in a sticky situation."

"Unfortunately, but I did get myself out of that jam in the end."

Lady Emma glanced into the distance before looking back at me. "I'll talk to Marlowe."

I reached out and squeezed her hand. "How very marvelous of you, darling."

CHAPTER 27

A CHEERY SUPPER

A more relaxed Lord Rutledge joined us for supper that evening. No wonder. A tremendous weight had been lifted from his shoulders. Not only had Robert's claim to the title been confirmed, but he'd been proven to have told the truth. I hoped that his relationship with Robert returned to their previous conviviality. Unfortunately, we still had to discover Freya Poole's murderer so that stress was bound to remain.

But our discovery had made the mood lighter. Hollingsworth spent a good part of the meal sharing amusing tales from his travels at sea. While Marlowe did not have the same wealth of adventures to draw upon, he told us about his early upbringing. His father, an envoy in China for the British government, had fallen in love and married a Eurasian lady. A year after their wedding, Marlowe had been born. His early upbringing was spent in Beijing. But after seven years, his father decided to return to England. There was a growing resentment against foreigners, and he felt it best to leave. And since Marlowe would be inheriting the title, it would be best for him to attend a British school.

"Did you ever return?" I asked.

"No. The Boxer Rebellion erupted in 1900. The uprising against foreigners caused many to flee for their lives. Mother was glad we were safe in England."

His parents were no longer alive. So I was curious what had happened to them. But Marlowe was such a private person, I did not wish to pry. He'd tell us if he wished us to know.

After supper, Lord Rutledge once more retired to his room, although this time in a happier mood. The rest of us proceeded to the billiards room. I'd never been an aficionado, but I knew the basic rules of the game. Lady Emma and I were happy enough to encourage the gentlemen. While I chose Robert, she cheered for Hollingsworth at first. But then during the next game, she switched to Marlowe.

"Hollingsworth, you have to get yourself a love interest."

"My dear Kitty. I have one. The sea. I miss her every damn day I'm away from her."

"Oh, such salty language," I exclaimed.

"I'm a sailor, remember? I know many salty words."

"Which we'll thank you to keep to yourself in front of the ladies, Hollingsworth," Robert said.

After two hours, I was ready to retire, as I could hardly keep myself awake. Neither could Lady Emma. So we linked arms and left the gentlemen to their port and cigars.

Annie helped me slip out of my dress and into a plain flannel nightgown. But it was comfortable and warm, and that was all I cared about. After my head hit the pillow, it took me but a moment to fall asleep. My mind, however, kept churning away because in the middle of the night I came wide awake.

Needing to tell Robert about the revelation I'd just dreamed up, I dashed through my dressing room, the bathroom we shared, and his dressing room to his bedroom door. I jiggled the doorknob, but it was locked. So I banged on the door. "Robert. Wake up. Robert!" I pounded some more.

Suddenly the door burst open. And there he was, bare chested, a sheet wrapped around the lower part of his body.

How odd. "Why are you dressed that way?"

"Why do you think?"

It took a moment or two for my not-yet-wide-awake brain to understand. "You sleep in the nude?"

He hiked a brow. He had a point. I should have at the very least suspected it.

If I were a virginal maiden—well, let's face it I was, but I knew things—I would have fainted, cried out, or at the very least blushed. I did none of those things. Instead, I stood there relishing the sight of him.

He scrubbed a hand across his face. "What do you want, Catherine?"

"You don't wear pajamas to bed?"

"Catherine, for the love of—"

I grinned. "Well, I'll have to take that off your Christmas gift list then."

"I want you to turn around and go back to your room. Now!"

He did not appreciate my humor, but I had something that would make him listen. "I know who killed Freya Poole."

"What?" That got his attention.

"Get dressed, and I'll explain it to you. Or"—I licked my lips—"you can come as you are."

"I'll get dressed."

I stood there waiting and waiting, but he didn't move. "Well?"

"I can't dress until you leave."

"Why?"

"Because you're standing in my dressing room. All my clothes are in there."

"Oh? All right." I turned around. "See you in a few minutes then."

"You might want to put on some proper clothes yourself," he yelled.

I twisted around and faced him. "I'm wearing a flannel nightgown that covers me from neck to foot. That's more cloth than I wear during the day."

"It's nightwear and, therefore, improper."

"If you think this is improper, wait until you see what I've planned for our wedding night," I tossed over my shoulder. Even from the Lady's Chamber, I heard him groan. So much for my promise to Mother to stop tempting him.

He kept me waiting fifteen minutes. Honestly, how long did it take for him to dress? It wasn't as if he was expected at the palace. Finally, after what seemed like forever, there was a knock on the dressing room door. "Enter."

He was wearing a pair of trousers and a shirt buttoned up to his neck. And he'd taken the time to brush his hair and shave.

I couldn't help but feel disappointed. "A shame."

"What?"

"I prefer you half naked. Or all naked. Either would do."

"You haven't seen me all naked."

"But I can use my imagination. And you do know there are periodicals that reveal all."

A look of horror spread about his face. "You haven't?"

I thought to tease him some more but decided against it. He would probably suffer an apoplexy if I did. "No. I have

166

not. I'm saving that special treat for our wedding night. Unless you want to show me a preview."

He rubbed two fingers up his wrinkled brow. "Who killed Freya Poole?"

I told him.

"Why do you think that?"

I told him that as well.

"You realize we have no proof."

"No, we don't. We'll just have to get him to admit it."

"And how do you plan to do that?"

"He has an Achilles Heel. We'll use it against him. Here's my plan." By the time I finished explaining it, the sun was cresting over the horizon, and I was growing drowsy. "I have to get some sleep. I'll leave you to arrange things."

"Very well. Shall I say goodnight again?"

"Yes, please."

He bent over to kiss me and that's when Annie opened the door. After one look, she giggled and shut the door.

"I can only imagine what the staff will think of this," I said.

"Do you care?" he asked.

"Not in the least."

And then he kissed me some more.

CHAPTER 28

A PLAN IS MADE

*H*ours later when I woke, I wasn't surprised it was past nine. Breakfast would have been served hours ago, so I rang for Annie, not only to help me dress but to bring something to eat. I was perishing for coffee as well as food.

She must have been expecting my summons for it didn't take long for her to arrive. "I brought your favorites," she said resting the tray on the round table in front of the fireplace. "A rasher of bacon, eggs, toast, scones, and clotted cream."

"Tell me you also brought coffee."

"Yes, miss."

"You're an angel sent from heaven, Annie." I sat down and promptly poured some of the fragrant brew into the cup. After adding sugar and cream, I took a sip and sighed. "Don't know what I'd do without it." As there was something I wished to discuss with her, I invited her to sit.

"Ta, miss."

I buttered a slice of toast and crunched into it. "Ummm. This butter tastes differently from the one back home."

"It's freshly churned."

"That explains it. And the strawberry jam?"

"Cook made a new batch just yesterday."

I wiped my mouth with a napkin after demolishing the rest of the toast. "Have you seen Lord Robert?"

She blushed. "His lordship has broken his fast but is now in the library with the other gentlemen."

"Splendid." He would be discussing the plan I suggested.

"Miss? I didn't tell anyone about what I saw this morn."

"Oh? I was rather hoping you would."

"Miss!" She said blushing.

"I'm teasing." After studying her for a second, I said, "You make an excellent lady's maid, Annie."

"Ta, Miss."

"Have you ever thought about working in London? We could use your services at Worthington Manor."

"I thank 'ee kindly, but I could never leave Chipping Bliss. My family is here."

"And family is everything. Well, now that I have demolished the food, I believe I shall dress for the day."

"Yes, Miss."

In no time at all, I changed into the cream-colored wool trousers and cowl neck navy Shetland jumper Mother had sent. I was grateful for them as the weather had turned colder. While I was slipping into leather boots, there was a knock on the door. Annie opened it to find one of the footmen on the other side.

"With Lord Robert's compliments, he would like Miss Worthington to join him in the library."

"Perfect timing!" As I was eager to see Robert after our late-night tête-à-tête, I took the stairs as quickly as I could and practically ran all the way to the library. And then there he was, as scrumptious as ever.

I strolled to his side and kissed his cheek. "Good morning, darling, I trust you slept well." I gazed up at him through my eyelashes.

He tweaked my chin, a tender gesture of his. "I did, minx."

I turned to find Hollingsworth, Marlowe and Lady Emma wearing different expressions. Hollingsworth was amused, Marlowe's jaw had dropped, and Lady Emma was biting down on her lips to keep from laughing.

Marlowe was not slow to voice his objection. "If you're going to make love, dash it all, do it in private."

"Says the man who jumped half-naked into the pond in St. James Park in full view of Kitty and me," Lady Emma said.

"I was a trifle inebriated at the time if you'll recall."

"A trifle? You were three sheets to the wind, Marlowe!" Lady Emma exclaimed. "If Robert hadn't stopped you, you would have done it in the buff."

Marlowe flashed her a satisfied masculine grin. "As I recall, you rather enjoyed the view."

"How would you remember? You were sloshed."

"There are things a chap doesn't forget." And with this pithy statement, he brought her hand to his lips and kissed it. Lady Emma did not object.

It seemed they had made their peace. Again. How long would it last this time? I had no idea.

Robert cleared his throat. "Now that we've exchanged pleasantries, could we get back to our discussion?"

"Yes, of course. Sorry to interrupt." Swinging my hips all the way to a wing back chair, I dropped into it.

Robert's gaze promised retribution. I could not wait.

By the end of an hour, we'd settled on our roles. Now all we had to do was play them out. And with the wedding only five days away, there was no time to waste. While Robert headed to the constabulary to inform Constable Merry-weather of our plan, Hollingsworth and Marlowe were dispatched to The Angry Swan. Lady Emma and I headed to Griselda's House of Beauty where I would avail myself of their treatments.

With today being Saturday, Griselda's was packed with customers. But the proprietor was not about to turn me away. Not when she could say the future Marchioness Rutledge had employed her services. We did have to wait, which was more than satisfactory. After all, we were there to seed the ground if you will.

I sighed. "I can't help but worry, Lady Emma."

"We'll make it back to London in time for your wedding, don't you worry. After all, the investigation is practically wrapped up."

"Is it really?" The lady next to me asked, a blonde whose dark roots were showing. More than likely, she was here for a touch-up.

"Yes. We're just waiting for one last bit of evidence to be verified, and then the culprit will be apprehended."

"Who was it?"

"Oh, I'm afraid I can't say. We wouldn't want the murderer to get wind of it, do we?"

"No. Of course not." She ditched her magazine and stood up. "Griselda. I'm sorry, but I just remembered something I had to do." And with that, she was gone.

Lady Emma and I made a concerted effort not to glance at each other. The rest of the afternoon went the same way. Some of the ladies sniffed with derision, but most couldn't wait to hear what we had to say.

When I paid the tab, Griselda asked, "Did our services prove satisfactory, Miss Worthington?"

"Indeed, they were. Next time I return to Castle Rutledge, I'll be sure to visit."

"I'm pleased to hear it. Feel free to bring your friends."

"I certainly will."

She leaned into me and whispered, "I'll be sure to get the word out."

"Oh?"

"About the investigation," she said tipping me a wink.

Obviously, Griselda was no fool.

By the time the five of us returned to Castle Rutledge, it was time for supper. So we had to wait until after the meal to conduct our discussion. Even though Hudson had not played a role in this part of the investigation, we included him. He may have a particular insight the rest of us lacked.

"Let's start with Robert, shall we?" I suggested. "What did Constable Merryweather have to say?"

"He agreed with our conclusion. But he thinks the murderer is too clever to reveal himself. He also fears we've overplayed our hand."

"How so?"

"Well, with you and Lady Emma spreading gossip at Griselda's House of Beauty and Marlowe and Hollingsworth doing the same at The Angry Swan, the killer might realize what we're up to."

"It was a gamble, I agree. But it was worth doing if it flushes him out." I turned to Hollingsworth. "So how did your sojourn to the pub go?"

"We acted like a couple of plonkers with nary a clever thought to our heads."

"And did they believe what you had to say?"

"I'll say, especially after Hollingsworth bought rounds for the house. And that was before he started singing one of his bawdy sea shanties."

I laughed. "I'd love to hear one."

"It's not for your ears, lass," Hollingsworth said. "It's

something sailors croon when they're so lonely they could cry."

Oh, my. Was he one of those sailors? He said he loved the sea, and I believed him. But when he was far away in foreign waters, did he miss everything that meant home?

The meeting broke up soon afterwards and we went our separate ways. Tomorrow we would discover if our plan had borne fruit.

CHAPTER 29

A THREATENING NOTE

*W*e woke the next morning to discover a note had been nailed to the castle's front gate. *Stop your meddling or a loved one will die.*

"Well, that's clear enough," Robert said when it was brought to him.

"It means he got the message," Hollingsworth said.

"We may have done more harm than good, though," I said.

"Explain."

"We let it be known we knew the murderer. If we leave without him being named, the villagers will spend the next decade looking at each other with suspicion. We can't allow for that to happen."

"What do you suggest we do?" Robert asked.

"I go to the vicarage and talk to Mrs. Reilly."

"What good would that do? She's not the killer."

"No. She's not. But she knows the murderer. I can get her

thoughts on him, so we can attempt something else. Don't worry. I won't name him."

"That's too dangerous a ploy, Catherine. He knows we'll try something else, and he's said he will kill a loved one. That's you. I won't allow you to put yourself in harm's way."

"What are you going to do, Robert? Tie me to a chair."

"If I have to."

"You won't darling. You're not that sort of man."

He grumbled.

"I'll be careful, I promise."

"If you don't return in an hour, I'll go after him myself. Proof or no proof."

"One way or another, we'll get it, Robert."

It was with more than a little trepidation that I traveled to the vicarage. Along the way, I planned what I would say. But it was all for naught. Mrs. Reilly was not there.

"Do you know where she is?" I asked the harried looking vicar.

"She didn't arrive this morning."

Alarm bells went off in my head. The killer's note said a loved one would die. We assumed it'd be one of us at the castle. But what if it was Mrs. Reilly? "Did you check her cottage?" I asked.

"I did. She wasn't there.

"Maybe Mister Lawson is aware of where she has gone."

"He knows no more than I do. He's searching for her as we speak."

"Where?"

"In the shops. Last night, she mentioned a need to replenish some foodstuffs. She might have headed to the grocer."

But a half hour later when Mister Lawson returned, the news was not good. "She's not in the village. Nobody has seen her."

"Time to get Constable Merryweather involved," I said.

Mister Lawson telephoned the constabulary with the news that Mrs. Reilly was missing. The constable rushed right over and got the details. I left them to it and returned to Castle Rutledge where Robert was waiting.

"I was giving you five more minutes and then I was heading to the vicarage. How did it go?"

"It didn't. Mrs. Reilly is missing," I said almost in tears. "Oh, Robert. He's taken her. I know he has."

"Did you alert Constable Merryweather?"

"The curate did. He rushed right over. They must be searching for her even as we speak."

"We'll offer our assistance." He summoned Benton and explained what had happened. "I need every able-bodied man who can be spared."

"Yes, Your Lordship. Of course." And off Benton went with a sprightlier step than I'd seen before.

"I'll help as well," I said.

"No, you will not. You will stay right here. Hollingsworth, Marlowe, and I will ride to the village with as many of the staff as possible. I don't want you involved in this, Catherine. Do you understand?"

"Fine."

"Promise you will stay here."

"I promise."

Benton was able to round up twenty men, half from the castle and the other half from the brewery. Within an hour they were on their way to the village in the Rolls, bicycles, carts, and one on a horse.

After they left, Lady Emma took me by the hand and sat me down. "He's right, you know. You're a more tempting target than Mrs. Reilly."

"But why her? She was no threat to him."

"Since when do murderers act rationally?"

The time passed slowly. While we waited, Mother telephoned. "Kitty, your wedding is in four days."

I explained the circumstances to her. "I promise, Mother, as soon as we find her, we'll be on the next train."

"What if you don't find her?"

"We'll leave. Nothing is going to stop me from marrying Robert."

Hours later, Robert and the Castle Rutledge search party returned.

"Any news?"

"No. I'm sorry. The entire village was searched door to door. She's not in Chipping Bliss."

She wasn't located the next day, but on the third she was found safe and sound wandering down the road, with no recollection of what happened to her. Everyone was thrilled she'd returned, but they all wondered what had happened. Unfortunately, we couldn't investigate her disappearance. We were leaving on the evening train.

But before departing Chipping Bliss, I wanted to ascertain for myself that Mrs. Reilly was of sound mind and body. The chauffeur drove Robert and me into the village. Robert so he could write his report at the constabulary. And me so I could see Mrs. Reilly at the vicarage. The driver had already taken Lord Rutledge, Marlowe, Hudson, and Lady Emma, to the Moreton on Marsh railway station. So only Robert, Hollingsworth, and I remained. Our bags were already stowed in the boot, so it was only a matter of finishing our business in the village.

Robert kissed me goodbye as I stepped off at the vicarage. "I'll return in an hour."

"Yes."

A much-relieved vicar opened the door. "Miss Worthington. Come to say goodbye?"

"I am and to see Mrs. Reilly."

"She's in the kitchen. You'd never know she'd gone through an ordeal."

I found her right where she'd always been in the kitchen stirring something in a pot.

"Mrs. Reilly. I was so worried about you." I embraced her tightly.

"No need to fret, dearie. I'm right as rain as you can see."

I scrutinized her closely. Indeed, she seemed as always. Still, I had to ask. "Are you sure?"

"Doctor Springwell gave me the once-over. He found nothing wrong."

"That's good to hear. Do you remember anything, anything at all about what happened?"

"None. The last memory I have is of me sitting right at this table making a list for the grocer. And then there I was walking down the road to the grocer. But two days had gone by."

"How very odd."

"'Tis. That's for sure. I have what you asked for." She fetched a carefully wrapped package and handed it to me. "You're leaving today?"

"Yes, on the evening train."

"I wish you and Lord Robert every happiness in the world."

"Thank you, Mrs. Reilly. Lord Robert is going to come by in about 30 minutes or so. Could you let him know I've gone to the apothecary? I need something to settle my stomach. I'm afraid I'm not a good train traveler and need something to settle my stomach."

"I surely will." I said goodbye to her and the vicar and went on my way.

CHAPTER 30

A VISIT TO THE APOTHECARY

The bell over the door rang as I entered the apothecary establishment. Mister Sloane was working behind the counter, as I imagined he did most days.

"Miss Worthington? Good afternoon. Is there something I can help you with?"

"Yes, there is. We're returning to London this evening. Train travel does not agree with me. I get rather anxious, you see. I was wondering if you had something that could help."

"Of course. I have just the thing. It'll take me a few minutes to prepare it. Is Lord Robert joining you?"

"Oh, he'll be along when he's done writing his report at the constabulary."

"His report?"

"Yes. We've identified Freya Poole's murderer. So, he wanted to memorialize what we've discovered. I have no idea how long he will be."

"Would you like some tea while you wait? I've just brewed

179

some of my special blend. It contains chamomile. It's sure to settle your nerves."

I beamed him my brightest smile. "That would be lovely, thank you."

"It you would like to take a seat. I won't be a moment." He pointed to a seating arrangement which consisted of two chairs upholstered in a blue damask. A small, round table rested between them. Two potted plans abutted the chairs.

After I settled myself in one of the seats, he excused himself. It took him little time to emerge from the back of the shop carrying a cup and saucer in his right hand. "I don't have milk or lemon, I'm afraid."

"That's fine. Thank you, Mister Sloane," I said accepting the tea.

"I'll go prepare your medicine then."

"I'll wait til the tea cools down a bit." It was so hot steam was rising from it.

"It should cool in a second."

He walked to the back of the shop. Ten minutes later, he returned with the medicine and handed the bottle to me with his left hand.

"What does it contain?"

"Laudanum. A couple of drops in a glass of water should ease your symptoms. Don't take more than that, though. You're likely to sleep round the clock."

"Oh, I wouldn't want that! I'm getting married tomorrow." I glanced at my wristwatch. "That is if we make the evening train."

"That would be a tragedy."

"Yes, it would. I love Robert with all my heart. I can't imagine life without him."

"I understand that sentiment."

"You love someone, don't you?"

"Yes. Yes, I do."

"But you're not in a position to marry."

"It can never be."

"The church, never mind the law, would frown upon such a marriage." He shot a surprised glance at me. "You are in love with Mister Lawson. That's why you murdered Freya Poole."

"That's a monstrous falsehood."

I placed the cup on the table with the tea untouched. "Which part? That you love Mister Lawson? Or that your murdered Freya Poole?"

"Both."

"What I've just spoken is the truth."

"Even if it were true, why would I murder her?"

"Because her gossip was hurting Mister Lawson and you couldn't have that. He'd suffered enough already at Upton when he was rumored to have fathered a child out of wedlock. She found out about your unrequited love for him. Something that wasn't hard to do. I saw the way you looked at him at the vicarage the day I came to visit. It was the gaze of a man in love."

"I do not—" He choked back tears.

I felt sorry for him. I really did. But I had to get him to admit what he'd done. "It's no good lying, especially when you were so very clever about the execution. You planned everything carefully so no blame could be laid at Mister Lawson's feet. Purporting to be a friend of his mother's, you sent him a note to draw him away."

"He would have recognized my handwriting."

"You're ambidextrous. You served me tea with one hand and offered the medicine with the other. You wrote the note with the hand you don't normally use for correspondence and prescriptions.

"You wanted him out of the way for more than that one reason, though. You needed the vicar to handle the details of the burial the day of the funeral. Given that he has a nervous disposition, you knew he would take sleeping powders the night before. So you purposefully provided him powders with twice the dosage."

"But they were unmarked papers."

"Easily achieved. You would not have put your mark on them. The vicar never even noticed as he took the medicine. After you'd ensured he'd sleep through the night and well into the day, it was ever so easy for you to slip into the church with Freya Poole's body and dress her in the vicar's vestments."

"How would I carry her from her house to the church? As you can see, I'm not a strong man."

"You used a wheelbarrow. There was one in the back of the vicarage. I noticed it when I went there one day. Of course, it fit right in with your plans. Once you carried Freya Poole to the church, you simply left it in the back of the building. Nobody would notice because it belonged there."

"You can't prove I did it."

I breathed out a hard sigh. "You're right, I can't."

"You admit it," he cried out in triumph.

"But that's not the only evil thing you've done. You also kidnapped Mrs. Reilly."

Still exulted, he said, "I wouldn't call it that, Miss Worthington."

"How did you manage it?"

"I visited the vicarage, shared a cup of tea with her, much as I'm doing with you." He glanced at my cup. "You haven't touched it."

"No. I have not." Nor would I. "What did you do to Mrs. Reilly?"

"When she was busy fetching scones from the oven, I slipped something into her tea. She became sweet as a lamb after that. I took her to a remote cottage I own, kept her there for two days. The drug would ensure she wouldn't remember a thing."

"Why did you take her?"

"To keep you and Lord Robert from discovering I was the murderer. I knew you'd be concerned enough about Mrs. Reilly's disappearance you would pause your investigation and search for her. With your wedding day set for tomorrow, you'd have to leave without reaching a conclusion. That fool Merryweather would never figure out things on his own. And I would get off scot free."

"Your scheme did not go as you planned. We determined you were the murderer."

"But, as you said, you have no proof." He grinned.

Rather than address his point, I said, "Have you thought what will happen if the murderer is not named?"

He shrugged. "Not really."

"Everyone in the village will come under suspicion including Mister Lawson."

He shot a furious glance at me. "He wasn't here. I made sure of that. And there were witnesses who saw him at his mother's house."

"During the day. But he has no alibi for that night. Upton is only a few miles from Chipping Bliss. He could have made his way here."

"How?"

"By bicycle. There was a full moon that night. The road was easily seen, and he is very familiar with it."

"Why would he kill Freya Poole?"

"For the same reason you did. She was spreading vicious rumors about him. He wanted to end them. And there was only one way to do that permanently."

"Andrew is a good person. Everyone knows that."

"And yet, he's been caught up in two scandals—one in Upton and another one right here in Chipping Bliss. As the saying goes, where there's smoke, there's fire." I allowed that to sink in before I said, "He's planning to leave, did you know that?"

His breath shorted. "That's a blatant lie," he screeched out.

"Not so. His mother told me. The village gossip has worn him down. He's applied for a position in London."

"He can't leave. He can't leave me." His eyes glowed with a maniacal light. He was obsessed with the curate to the point of madness.

"I'm afraid that's beyond your control. You have no hold on him. He doesn't love you."

"I never expected love, only friendship," he sniveled. "That's all I wanted from him."

"You won't even have that when he's gone, Mister Sloane."

"I can't live without him. I can't."

"I'm afraid you'll have to."

He bared his teeth at me. "No, I won't." He grabbed the cup of tea he'd given me and gulped it down in one long pull. And then he smiled in triumph.

Horrified by his action, I asked, "What was in that tea, Mister Sloane?" I'd suspected something that would render me unconscious to give him time to get away. But now?

"Hemlock. The same I gave to Freya. Rather poetic, don't you think?" He stiffened up. His pupils dilated. His mouth twisted in a rictus of pain.

The door to the apothecary shop burst open. Robert, Hollingsworth, Constable Merryweather, and Sergeant Purdy rushed in.

"Catherine. For the love of God," Robert said. "What the blazes are you doing here?"

"Getting a confession from Mister Sloane," I whispered. I couldn't exult in it, not with what was happening to the apothecary.

"Did he confess?" Constable Merryweather asked.

"Yes, he did," I said as Mister Sloane's gurgle of death filled the space. His head dropped forward as he breathed his last breath.

"What happened?" Robert asked.

"The cup contained hemlock, the same poison he gave to Freya Poole. He served it to me. I knew better than to drink it. After I explained we knew everything, he took the cup and drank it all."

Constable Merryweather checked the apothecary's pulse. "He's gone." He turned to Sergeant Purdy. "Go telephone Doctor Springwell from the constabulary. He'll need to pronounce him."

With a nod, the sergeant left in a rush.

Robert picked me up from the chair and embraced me. "I died a thousand deaths when Mrs. Reilly told me where you'd gone."

"I can handle myself, Robert."

"He fed you poison!"

"Which I did not drink." The church clock struck six times. "Oh, no. We'll never make the last train."

CHAPTER 31

ALL'S WELL THAT ENDS WELL

*T*hankfully, the Rolls Royce was right outside, so all Robert, Hollingsworth and I had to do was jump into it. The chauffeur rushed through Chipping Bliss. Same as the day we arrived, it appeared deserted. But then it was suppertime. Everyone was probably enjoying their evening meals.

Robert glanced at his watch. "We're not going to make it. The last train departs at 6:31. It's fifteen after now."

"Maybe it'll be late."

"Not likely to, Miss," the chauffeur. "That train runs like clockwork."

I sighed. "We'll drive on to London then." I was not going to miss our wedding day.

On a cloud of dust, the Rolls pulled into the railway station. The three of us jumped out of the automobile as a porter rushed over to pile our luggage and a wooden box into his cart.

"What's in that thing?"

"Castle Rutledge Reserve Whiskey. I wasn't going home without it."

Suddenly, a loud whistle blew. Miracle of miracles the train was at the platform. "It hasn't left."

"Come on!" Robert grabbed my hand, and we took off at a run. When one of my shoes fell off, I reached for it. But he was having none of it, "Leave it!"

I hobbled two steps before he picked me up and raced with me to the train.

As it turned out, there was no rush. Half the village had lined themselves up and down the platform. The other half stood in front of the train on the tracks, blocking its path.

Needless to say, the conductor was not pleased. "Get out of the way, you blighters, I have a schedule to keep."

"They held up the train! For us!" I said.

"Miss Worthington," Mrs. Collins, the castle housekeeper stepped forward with a bouquet of flowers. Where on earth had she obtained them? It was October, after all. "From the castle staff, Miss. We wish you and Lord Robert a happy wedding day."

"Thank you, Mrs. Collins."

"Stop shilly-shallying about and get on board," the conductor yelled from the front of the train.

As a young lad ran up with my missing shoe, a laughing Robert and I jumped on the train steps. Hollingsworth was already on board. The conductor blew the train whistle, and the train came to life. Hanging on to Robert with one hand, I waved goodbye to the cheering crowd with the other. But soon the train tracks curved, and the throng disappeared from view.

"Get in here, Catherine," Robert said pulling me up the steps. "I don't want you falling off the train before I have a chance to marry you."

Laughing, I threw my arms around him. "That would be a tragedy."

At the front of the car, Hudson was waiting for us. "Lord Rutledge is in a private compartment. Nigel is attending to him. Your supper will be served in the dining car after you refresh yourselves."

We were rather windblown. "Thank you, Hudson."

It took but a few minutes to right ourselves, and soon we were enjoying a delicious chop with fried potatoes, bread and butter, and strong cups of coffee in the dining car. Once we finished, we stopped at Lord Rutledge's compartment.

"How are you, Sir?" Robert asked.

"I don't intend to die before I see you wed, boy, so stop worrying about me," he said in his usual, irascible manner which I took to mean he was feeling fine.

"Yes, Sir."

"I trust the villain has been found."

"You'll need a new apothecary," Robert said without offering any further explanation. There'd be time enough to do that at a later time.

"Will I, by George? Well, should be easy enough to find one in London. I'll leave that chore to you."

"Yes, Sir."

"Now, leave me alone. I need my beauty rest."

I chuckled as he intended me to.

The rest of the journey did not take long. We arrived at Paddington shortly before ten. As Robert wished to escort Lord Rutledge home, we only enjoyed a brief goodbye. But I would see him soon enough. "The next time we see each other . . ." I whispered breathlessly.

"Will be at the church when I will finally make you mine," Robert answered.

Neville, our family's chauffeur, stood by the open door of the Rolls waiting to take me home. But I had one more thing to do before parting from my fiancé. I tugged on his tie and kissed him. "Dream of me, Inspector."

A soft smile bloomed across his lips as I slipped into the Rolls.

"How is everything at home, Neville?" He might be the chauffeur, but he knew everything that went on at Worthington House.

"It's a madhouse, Miss."

"That's what I thought." I girded my loins for what was to come.

CHAPTER 32

DEARLY BELOVED

*M*y wedding day dawned bright and clear but cold. It seemed as if I'd just laid my head on the pillow when I was awakened by Grace, my maid. "Coffee, Miss?"

"You are an angel sent from heaven."

"Yes, Miss. Cook sent up your breakfast. Mrs. Worthington thought a light meal would be best."

At this late date, she was still worried I wouldn't fit into my wedding gown. Although what could be done about it now, I had no idea.

"Your bath will be ready in fifteen minutes."

Which meant I would need to gulp down the coffee and scarf down the food.

"Miss Angelique and her assistant have arrived. They will dress you as soon as you're ready."

"What time is it, Grace?"

"Eight, Miss."

"Oh, goodness." The ceremony was scheduled for eleven. There was no time to waste. Fifteen minutes later I was in the claw-foot tub. After emerging from it, Grace styled my hair into the curls Robert loved. I applied a light maquillage, leaving off the lipstick until I was dressed. Once that was done, Angelique helped me into the undergarments she'd especially designed and, of course, my wedding gown.

"Mrs. Worthington wanted to let you know your attendants are dressed and the photographer is waiting downstairs," Grace said.

"Are we on schedule?"

"Just, Miss." It was thirty past nine. A half hour was allotted for the photographs in Worthington House before we left for the church.

"And now for the cap and veil," Angelique said. Before I could ask, she said, "We made the changes you requested."

"Thank you, Angelique. It means a lot to me."

Once she was done arranging it, the delicate lace veil flowed from my head to the floor. It was one of the most beautiful things I had ever worn.

I took a deep breath and stepped into the hallway. Mother was waiting with tears in her eyes. "My beautiful girl."

"Thank you, Mother."

"A little lipstick wouldn't hurt, dear."

"Oh, heavens, I forgot."

Grace fetched the shade I'd chosen along with a hand mirror. It was with a not quite steady hand, I applied it across my lips.

Once I'd done so, I turned to my three bridesmaids. "What do you think?"

"Oh, Kitty," Margaret said. "You are luminous."

"Thank you, dear sister. Lady Emma?"

"I've never seen you so happy."

I was that. In but a few hours, I would marry the love of my life.

"You make a most beautiful bride, Kitty," Lady Lily said. "I can't wait to see the look on Robert's face."

I pressed her hand. "Neither can I."

Father waited for me at the top of the stairs, so overcome with emotion he couldn't say a word but simply stared at me.

"Well, Father?"

"You look beautiful, Kitty girl."

"Thank you."

"Don't dawdle, dears," Mother said. "The photographer is waiting."

Father extended his arm. I curled my hand around it and together we descended the stairs.

At the bottom, we were greeted by the oohs and aahs of the staff who broke into a round of applause.

"Best of wishes, Miss Worthington."

"Many blessings to you and Lord Robert."

"May the sun never set on your happiness."

"Thank you all," I said.

The photographs took more time than I thought they would. But after forty five minutes, they were finally done, and we were on our way to St. George's at Hanover Square. It took four Rolls Royces to transport the wedding party. Mother, Richard, and Lady Mellie in one, Margaret, Lady Lily, and Lady Emma in another, Sebastian, Ned, and Mister Sharif in a third, and Father and me in the fourth. Hollingsworth, as best man, was responsible for getting Robert to the church.

A crowd of curious onlookers who'd gathered outside the church broke into applause as the automobiles arrived. Of course, members of the press were there as well. They couldn't be avoided. As prominently as Robert and I had been featured front and center in their papers, they were not likely to miss our wedding day.

Father and I slowly made our way up the steps of the church with only a minor snag. The wedding veil got temporarily caught on my heel, but Lady Emma freed it without any damage. We were greeted by a church official who took us to a retiring room where we could make any last-minute adjustments. And then it was time.

As I hadn't been able to make the rehearsal, Mother had explained the order of the procession to me. Lady Lily would go first, followed by Lady Emma. Margaret, as my matron of honor would precede Father and me. The music swelled signaling the start and one by one the bridesmaids proceeded down the aisle. And then after a temporary pause, Wagner's Bridal March began to play and everyone in the church came to their feet.

"Ready?" Father asked.

"Yes. I love you, Father."

"I love you, Kitty." I looked straight ahead to where Robert stood his back to me, with Hollingsworth next to him. I knew Robert wouldn't glance in my direction. He would wait to see me until I was standing next to him. It seemed forever before we finally made it to the front of the altar where the priest waited for us, but we finally did.

As I took one last step to stand next to Robert, he turned toward me. The love and emotion in his eyes, dear God, I could only hope he could see the same in mine.

"Who gives this woman away?" the priest asked.

"Her mother and I do," Father said. And then he put my hand in Robert's. "Love her as she's meant to be loved, son."

"I will, Sir." As Father stepped back to join Mother, Richard, and Lady Mellie in the front pew, Robert raised my hand to his lips and kissed it. "You look beautiful, Catherine."

"Thank you, darling. I love you."

"Not as much as I love you."

"Do you like the veil?" An odd sort of question to ask at such a moment. Still, he took it in stride.

"I love it."

"It's your mother's. She never got to wear it. I wanted to honor her memory when I married her son."

With a hand that trembled, Robert cupped my cheek. "Thank you, my love."

The priest cleared his throat to gain our attention. We gave it to him.

"Dearly Beloved."

If someone asked me what happened the rest of the ceremony, I would honestly say I didn't remember most of it. But I must have said and done the right things because he was finally pronouncing us man and wife. "Those whom God hath joined together let no man put asunder. Robert, you may kiss your bride."

Two years ago at my Swiss Finishing School, I'd learned the proper deportment of a bride at such a moment. A chaste kiss and a soft smile. Needless to say, that did not happen. Our kiss was incendiary leaving no one in doubt of our desire for each other.

"Lord and Lady Robert," the priest said with a heavy sigh, "I suggest you leave that for this evening when you're alone. Your guests are waiting."

"Yes, of course," I said peeling my lips from Robert.

"Our apologies," my newly-minted husband said with a grin.

And then, to the glorious music of Mendelssohn's Wedding March, we walked up the aisle into the rest of our lives.

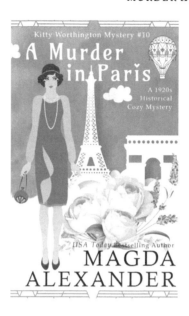

MARRIED AT LAST, Kitty and Robert are happily looking forward to their honeymoon in Paris. But, wouldn't you know it? Things don't go quite according to plan.

A honeymoon in Paris. Idyllic days and nights. It couldn't be more perfect. Until somebody dies.

October 1924. After their magical wedding, **Kitty Worthington** and her husband, **Inspector Robert Crawford Sinclair,** head to Paris for their honeymoon. Art museums, haute couture, French cuisine. Wondrous nights. It's everything Kitty has always dreamed of and more. But then a body drops putting a damper on things.

At least this time, it's a matter for the French police. There's no need for Kitty and Robert to get involved. Things change, however, when a dear friend becomes the chief suspect, and she begs Kitty for help. Unable to walk away, she and Robert agree to investigate.

As they desperately search for clues, they discover a tortuous trail that leads from the Eiffel Tower to the Champs-Élysées and the Sacré-Cœur Basilica. With time running out, the solution eludes them, until they realize the answer is to be found in the most macabre place of all, the Paris Catacombs.

Filled with intrigue, glamour, and more than a soupçon of humor, **A Murder in Paris, Book 10 in The Kitty Worthington Mysteries**, is a captivating historical cozy mystery sure to delight lovers of Agatha Christie and Downton Abbey alike.

Capture the QR code below with your phone camera, and you will be taken to the **A Murder in Paris** Amazon Book Page.

～

WOULD you like to read Kitty and Robert's wedding night epilogue? A great dash of fun with a bit of heat. Capture the image below with your phone camera to download it.

ISBN-13: (EBook) 978-1-943321-27-8

ISBN-13: (Paperback) 978-1-943321-28-5

Hearts Afire Publishing

Made in United States
Troutdale, OR
05/03/2024

19638253R00116